# THE SETUP

## A SINGLE IN SEATTLE NOVEL

## KRISTEN PROBY

&
AMPERSAND
PUBLISHING, INC.

The Setup
A Single in Seattle Novel
By
Kristen Proby

THE SETUP

A Single in Seattle Novel

Kristen Proby

*I need to send a big thank-you to my childhood friend, Aubrey Hanson, who has worked at the Grand Ol' Opry for many years and generously gave me the inside scoop on what happens behind the scenes at the Opry. Thank you so much, Aubrey!*

*Any mistakes or discrepancies are on me.*

With the Single in Seattle series quickly growing, and the size of the entire family, I figured it was time to include a who's who in this huge world, listed by family. Please know that this may contain spoilers for anyone who hasn't read all of the books, but it's a great reference for those who want to make sure they read about everyone.

**The Williams Family**

**Parents:** Luke and Natalie – {Come Away With Me}

**Olivia 'Liv' Williams** – Works for her father's production company, Williams Productions, as the lead costume designer. Married to Hollywood celebrity **Vaughn Barrymore**. – {The Secret}

**Keaton Williams** – Restores rare vehicles. With country music star **Sidney Sterling** (Siblings are Gray and Maya Sterling). – {The Setup}

**Haley Williams** – Book to come.

**Chelsea Williams** – Book to come.

**Parents: Mark and Meredith Williams** – {Breathe With Me}

**Lucy Williams** – Book to come.

**Hudson Williams** – Book to come.

**Aunt & Uncle: Samantha and Leo Nash** – {Rock With Me}

No Children.

**The Montgomery Family**

**Parents: Isaac and Stacy Montgomery** – {Under the Mistletoe With Me}

**Sophie Montgomery** - Nutritionist and social media influencer. Married to **Ike Harrison**, quarterback for Seattle professional football team. – {The Score}

**Liam Montgomery** – Book to come.

**Parents: Jules (Montgomery) and Nate McKenna** – {Fight With Me}

**Stella McKenna** – Interior designer. Married to attorney **Gray Sterling** (Siblings are Sidney and Maya Sterling). – {The Scandal}

**Parents: Caleb and Brynna Montgomery** – {Safe With Me}

**Maddie Montgomery** – Accountant. Married to **Dylan**, a travel writer. – {The Scramble}

**Josie Montgomery** – Nurse. Married to **Brax Adler**, a musician. – {The Surprise}

**Michael "Drew" Montgomery** – Professional Football Coach. Book to come.

**Parents: Will and Meg Montgomery** – {Play With Me}

**Erin Montgomery** – Book to come.

**Zoey Montgomery** – Book to come.

**Parents: Matt and Nic Montgomery** – {Tied With Me}

**Abby Montgomery** – Book to come.

**Finn Montgomery** – Book to come.

**Parents: Dominic and Alecia Salvatore** (Montgomery brother) – {Forever With Me}

**Emma Salvatore** – Book to come.

# PLAYLIST

All songs are written and produced by Josiah and Rachel Holien, especially for this book. The songs can be found on Spotify.

1. Life in the Slow Lane
2. Moon Shine
3. Good Girls Gone Bad
4. Little Miss

# PROLOGUE

## KEATON

"I hate being so far away from you." I'm lying flat on my back, staring at the ceiling of my bedroom, my phone pressed to my ear, trying to hear every little detail on the other end of the line. I've been dating Sabrina Tuttle, only the hottest actress in Hollywood, long distance for three months.

Three *agonizing* months.

"I know, babe," comes the throaty response from her. She has a voice that can make me hard in three-point-seven seconds. "But you're going to come down and see me next month, right?"

"That's the plan. My dad has some business down there, and I'm going to come with him."

Of course, I haven't told *him* that yet, but it shouldn't be a problem. He let me go down with him three months ago when I met Sabrina. She's been an actress since she was a kid, and I'd had a crush on her for a couple of years. I've seen all of her movies. So, when I met her at a lunch deal my dad took me to, I was a little tongue-tied at first.

But she was flirty and funny, and we hit it off. The more I talk with her, the more I love her. Not only is she hot, but she's also *smart*.

"God, why does my dad have to be so set on the whole *living in Seattle* thing?"

"I hear he doesn't like the limelight very much," she says.

"He hates it. Still, though, he goes to LA for work all the damn time. We might as well live there. Then I could see you whenever I want. Hey, speaking of seeing you, let me just video call you."

"Oh, that's okay," she says in a hurry. "I don't look great right now."

"You *always* look great," I insist.

"That's not true." I can hear the smile in her voice, and I want to see her so badly I can taste it. I want to *touch* her. I've only kissed her, but I'm hoping that changes next month because I'm ready to be with her in *every* way possible.

"Really, let's just talk. I love your voice. We can video chat tomorrow."

"Yeah, okay. I guess that's fine. What are you doing tomorrow?"

"I have to be on set early, and I'll be working all day again. This one is a busy shoot because they're trying to get it done quickly. The network wants to air it sooner rather than later."

"I'm so proud of you," I tell her, the words rushing out of my mouth. "You're just badass, Sabrina."

"Thanks. That means a lot, Keaton. Well, I'd better go. I'm exhausted, and I have that early start tomorrow."

"Right, you need to rest. Sleep well, babe."

"You, too. Bye." She hangs up, and I let the phone fall to the bed beside me. Why *can't* we live in LA? Sure, we'd all have to change schools, but that's not really a big deal. I'll have to talk to my dad about it later.

Because I want to be with Sabrina, no matter what.

"DUDE." My best friend, Mason, wraps his arm around my neck as we walk down the hallway at school, but he's not grinning. He looks grim as fuck.

"What?"

"I need to show you something, and it's going to really piss you off."

I scowl and look around to see that a few kids are watching us with interest.

"Let's go out to my car, then. Too many eyes here."

He nods, and we walk out the double doors that lead to freedom. The school day is over, and it's Friday, so that means I don't have to be back here for two fucking days.

They'll go by too damn fast. I fucking hate school. The quicker June rolls around and I'm out of here, the better.

Mason and I climb into the 1967 Camaro I've been restoring, and he pulls his phone out of his pocket and takes a deep breath.

"Dude, just show me what's up. You're being dramatic."

"Yeah, well, it's not good. Just remember, I'm only the messenger, okay?"

"Show me."

He taps his phone, then passes it to me, and I scowl.

"Is that Sabrina?"

"Yeah."

I narrow my eyes. It looks like she's sitting on a couch with a guy, cuddled up to him. They're kissing, and it makes my stomach roll.

"This must be old footage."

"I don't think so. Keep watching."

They pull away long enough to sip some drinks. It could be beer, but I'm not sure. The person doing the recording starts to talk.

"So, Sabrina, are you still stringing that kid of Luke Williams along?"

She smirks. She clearly doesn't know she's being recorded.

"He's a nice boy," is all she says as she shrugs carelessly.

*Nice.* Not exactly the way I'd like to be described.

"You're totally playing him," the guy she's snuggled up to says with a laugh. "Just to get in good with his dad."

"Hey, a girl's gotta do what a girl's gotta do. Who doesn't want to star in a Williams film? This could be my ticket to the next level."

"And in the meantime, you get to dick around with his kid," the recorder says. I can tell by the tone of his voice that he doesn't approve.

And so can she.

"What do *you* care? He's fine. He's just a boy. And if I can get to his dad this way, it's fine."

"Do you just want to star in a film, or do you *want* his dad?" the recorder asks. "I know you've always had a crush on Luke."

"Maybe both." Her smile is sly, and although she's only seventeen, she knows exactly what she's doing.

"That's enough." I stop the recording and pass it back to Mason, who hasn't said a fucking word. "Where did you get that shit?"

"It was posted online," he says and then cringes when my head whips around, and I stare at him in horror. "I *know*. It's on the socials, and some tabloids have picked it up."

"Fuck me sideways." I drag my hand down my face. Jesus, I'm such a goddamn fool. Why did I believe all of her bullshit? I know better. I'm related to someone famous, and I know the score when it comes to people

5

in LA, but I fell for her shit, hook, line, and sinker. "I'm an idiot."

"Nah, you just got played, man. It happens."

"Not like this. I'll drop you off at home."

We're silent as we drive through the suburb of Seattle, where we both live, and I pull into his driveway.

"If you want to talk about it, just text me," Mason says as he opens the door. "I'll be around all weekend."

"Thanks, man."

I watch as he climbs out and slams the door, and then I blow out a breath.

I thought Sabrina was different from other superficial girls. Since puberty, I've dealt with girls wanting to date me because of who my family is. I'm part of the Montgomery clan, which means that I have pro footballers, rock stars, and all kinds of cool people in my family. And I love them. But kids are starstruck and take it too fucking far.

I thought Sabrina would *understand* that, and she'd be different because she lives the same damn life.

And yet, here we are.

I'm mortified. Yeah, I'm disappointed, and my heart is bruised, but more than that, I'm embarrassed. I was too smitten with her to see the writing on the wall.

Jesus, was she at that party *last night*, and that's why she didn't want to video chat?

"Fuck me," I mutter as I park in front of my house and walk inside.

"Hey, sweetheart," Mom says with a big, happy

smile, the way she always does when we get home from school. "Want a snack?"

"Nah, I'll be in my room."

She frowns, but I don't stop to explain. I just hurry to my room and shut the door, drop my bag on the floor, and feel like punching a wall.

Maybe I'll go down to the workout room in the basement that Dad had put in when I was a little kid.

Yeah, that's what I need. To sweat. To hit something.

To just exhaust myself so I forget how fucking terrible my life is right now.

I quickly change and then jog down to the basement. Surprisingly, Dad's already there, doing pull-ups.

"Hey," is all he says as I move to the treadmill, set it for a fast speed, and begin to run.

Maybe I can just run away from all the bullshit that's just been unloaded on me in the last hour. God, I thought I loved that girl.

What a fucking joke.

I run until my lungs are screaming and the sweat pours off of me.

Then, I get off the treadmill, and, while wiping my face with a towel, I walk to the punching bag and take a turn there, not even giving my lungs much of a rest.

If my body hurts, I don't have time to think about today's humiliation.

When my arms feel like rubber, and my lungs feel like they might just give out on me altogether, I turn to get some water and find my dad sitting on a nearby bench, watching me with sober blue eyes.

"You know."

He nods and passes me a bottle of water. "I know."

I crack the lid on the water bottle, tip it back, and down the entire thing, then toss it into the recycling bin. "Awesome. I'll add it to my list of things to feel humiliated over."

"You shouldn't feel that way. And, if it makes you feel any better, she'll be hard-pressed to find work for a *very* long time. She fucked with my family. Now, I squish her like a bug."

My eyes turn to his. I feel perilously close to tears, and that just pisses me off more, but the intense look of anger and protectiveness on my dad's face makes me feel a little better. "Am I too old to let my dad fight my battles?"

"You're my minor son, and if you think that I'll let what she pulled slide by, you're mistaken. This isn't your fault, Keaton. You found a girl that you liked, you trusted her, and she betrayed you. It's not unheard of when you're a teenager."

"Yeah, except she's famous, *you're* famous, and that means your name is all over the goddamn gossip media, which is exactly what you're always trying to avoid. It's just one more thing for people to talk about, all because I was stupid enough to fall for her shit."

"Why don't you sit down, and we'll talk about this."

"No." My mind made up, I shake my head and peel

my sweat-soaked shirt over my head and ball it up in my hands. "I don't want to talk about it. Ever. It's done. There will be no more dating celebrities. You've had it right all along. I want nothing to do with that life. I'll just fade into the woodwork, and everyone can just forget about me."

"Keaton."

But I don't turn around as I march to the door, yank it open, and head back upstairs.

This is a closed subject. And I won't make this same mistake *ever* fucking again.

# CHAPTER 1

## SIDNEY

*I*'ve had a sick feeling in my stomach for a month.

Maybe longer.

Sure, I've been on tour all over the United States and Canada for the past year, and I've had a blast singing my ass off for thousands of people, but my sixth sense has been screaming at me that something isn't right.

And that bitch is rarely wrong.

I *know* the numbers for this tour are down from the last one. Record sales are also down, and I wasn't nominated for any awards for the new album this year.

Like I told my agent, I just need to write a better album next year. I've already got some ideas for that, and I've been setting up sessions with some friends to collaborate on songwriting now that I'm back in Nashville.

So, things might not be as great as they've been in the past, in regard to my career, but I'll get it back on track.

I know I will. I just need some rest.

Last night in LA was the last night of the tour, and after a couple of hours doing meet and greets and celebrating with my band and crew, I flew through the night to get back to Nashville. I'm so damn exhausted I feel like I could sleep for a month. Maybe longer. I need a massage and a full day of pampering.

I need a damn day off.

"Thanks, Mike," I say with a smile as my driver turns into my driveway on the outskirts of Nashville. He's been on tour with me since the very first one, ten years ago, driving me around all the strange cities as if they're his hometowns, and I like having him on my team. He's almost like a bonus dad to me, and I trust him implicitly. I know that no matter what I say in this car, nothing will ever be repeated.

Trust is the most important thing in the world to me.

"You did a damn good job, Sid," he says, watching me in the rearview mirror as he drives the black car down my driveway and comes to a stop just steps from the front door. I can't help but notice the shiny red Jaguar parked nearby. "Now, get some rest before you dive head-first back into work."

"Yes, sir. Go enjoy some time with your family and thank them for letting me borrow you for a while." I wink at him and push out of the car. My bags and belongings have all been delivered to the house already this morning, and I'm pretty sure my housekeeper, Wendy, has everything put away by now.

Wendy doesn't live with me, but she stops by a few times a week to make sure I have groceries and to tidy up the house. I trust her completely, as well, and I count my blessings for her every day. I don't know what I'd do without her.

"Honey, I'm home," I call out as I push inside and set my Fendi handbag on the foyer table, then kick off my shoes and pad across the tile floor further into the house. "Wendy? Is Annie here? I think that's her car parked out front. She told me she got a new one last week—Oh."

I stop when I see Annie sitting on my couch, casually drinking coffee, as if she does it every day.

She doesn't. This is only the third time she's been at my house since we've been working together. The first time was to tell me in person that I'd signed my first record deal.

The second was about three years ago when I'd been asked to tour with Reba.

"The only time you come to my house is when you have good news."

"Welcome home," Wendy says from the kitchen when Annie just grins at me. "Would you like some coffee?"

13

"Just water for me," I reply and drop onto the couch across from Annie. "You don't exactly look happy."

Annie sighs and sets her mug on the coffee table, then drags her hand down her face as Wendy passes me a tall glass of ice water with cucumber floating in it.

Wendy's fancy like that.

"I'll be upstairs, refreshing your linens," Wendy says in that breezy, everything-is-under-control way she has and bustles out of the room. "Let me know if you need anything."

"Thanks, Wendy."

Annie waits for Wendy to ascend the staircase before she sighs again and pins me with her sharp, brown eyes.

"Just say it."

"Okay, your label isn't going to offer you a new contract."

I blink at her. This isn't what I expected *at all.*

Before I can say anything, Annie stands and paces the living room, clearly not any happier with the situation than I am.

"The last album didn't perform," she says. "The tone of the songs and the content just wasn't what fans love from you, and it didn't sell even close to what they expected."

"They gave me some liberties with it, and, granted, I tried some new things. But damn, Annie, fans can't expect me to sing the same songs, over and over again."

"Oh, but they can, and they do." Her face is grim as

she turns to me once again. "The tour did about as well as the album. You saw the empty seats every night, Sid."

Yeah, I saw them. I tried my damndest to ignore them, but I saw them.

"It showed the label that you're just *not* a headliner, and in this business, if you have even one flop, they move on to the next artist. There are a thousand singers behind you that the label will record, and you know it."

"What do I do now?" I press my fingers into my eyes, trying to ease the headache that's set up residence in my forehead as I swallow down the panic. "Do we shop for a new label?"

"I think you need a break."

My eyes pop open, and I stare at Annie as if she just suggested I swim naked in the shark-infested ocean.

"I can't. I have to stay relevant. I have to stay in people's minds. Otherwise, I'm done, Annie."

"Not necessarily."

"Name *one* female artist who took time off and came back stronger than before."

Her lips twist as she thinks it over. "Trisha Yearwood."

"I'm not married to Garth." I stand and push my hands through my hair in agitation. "Fuck, Annie."

"Listen, I know this isn't what you want to hear. I'm *sorry* that the album didn't sell as well as the others. But, Sid, you've been working your ass off for a long time without a break. No one can maintain that level of work forever. Take a year off, rest, put on ten pounds."

"Oh, yeah, that'll be great. I won't fit into any of my stage costumes, and then the tailors will yell at me, and it'll be all over the tabloids that I have a food addiction."

"You're thin. The bags under your eyes have bags. Honey, you're not even *close* to thirty yet. You're too damn young to look this...*old*."

"I just came off tour, for Christ's sake!"

"The fifth one in a row. You release an album every single year. No one can expect you to continue at that pace."

I'm shaking now as I slowly sink back onto the couch and blow out a long breath.

"Annie, country music is my life. I've been at this for years, like you said, and I'm still only a mid-level artist. I feel like I'm fighting for my life here."

"For what? Honey, you've had an excellent, respectable career. You've won CMAs, you've toured with legends, and you've written songs that are beloved. Hell, you even had a Grammy nomination. That's more than most people even dream of."

"And yet, here I am, getting the axe from my label, and my agent is telling me to quit."

"No." She marches over to me and takes my shoulders in her hands. "No, Sid. I'm not telling you to quit. I'm telling you to *rest*. Write some music, collaborate with friends, and take a fucking vacation. You've been all over the globe, and you've only seen the insides of stadiums. Go sit on a beach somewhere and have a sexy man bring you drinks, then fuck his brains out."

I can't help but bark out a laugh at that.

"I'm going to book interviews for you, magazine spreads, and photo shoots so you're not completely out of sight and out of mind. And in those interviews, you tell them that you're writing the next album, and it's the best work you've ever done."

"Annie." I feel the tears come, partly from exhaustion and partly because I'm officially terrified. "This career is all I want. I've given up everything else to have it."

"I know." Annie's not a touchy-feely type, but she pulls me in for a hug. "I know, sweetie. You take some time to rest, and then you're going to make the biggest comeback in country music history, I promise you."

"You'd better be right, or I'll hire a new agent."

"Psh." She pulls away and shakes her head. "You would *never*. Sid, you have to make people *want* more from you. You always put new music out there so quickly that you don't give them time to miss you. Make them miss you."

"Maybe I should cover that Sam Hunt song." I blow out a breath. "Fine. I *am* tired, so I'll take a little time off. But you get me those interviews and shoots. I don't want to disappear entirely."

"Absolutely not. No way. Now, go get a massage and take a nap. Get a facial while you're at it."

"You know, you're *so* good for my ego."

Now she laughs and pats my cheek. "If I can't be honest with you, who can? I'll be in touch next week."

"Next week? Why not tomorrow?"

"Because you're resting, remember? Jesus, Sidney, learn to relax a little."

With that, she shakes her head, reaches for her bag, and walks out the front door.

I don't have a label.

*Jesus.*

Numbly, I climb the steps to my bedroom. As I suspected, my clothes have been unpacked, washed, and put away by the amazing Wendy. The bedroom smells like freshly laundered sheets and sunshine.

My house in the suburbs of Nashville isn't huge, but it's all mine. After that tour with Reba, I was able to buy it outright, and I snatched up that opportunity and remodeled the old house to make it my own.

I converted one of the bedrooms into a large closet and dressing room, and I walk in there now to change into pajama shorts and a tank, then walk back into the bedroom, peel back the covers on my king-size bed, and slip inside.

If I'm going to get my career back, I have to get some rest first. Then, I'm going to kick some ass and show that label that they made a *huge* mistake.

"Welcome home," my soon-to-be sister-in-law, Stella, says in my ear. My brother started seeing, and then living with, Stella a little over a year and a half ago, and although Gray is one of my favorite people in the world, his fiancée is quickly moving up the ladder to join him at the top.

I might even like her *more* than I like my brother.

Of course, I would never tell him that.

"Thanks." I yawn and check the time. "Shit, I slept almost all day."

"Not surprising. Your shows are super physical. I had no idea you played guitar, danced around, and did all the other things you did in concert. Thanks again for the seats here in Seattle, by the way. We had a blast."

"You're welcome. I'm glad everyone liked the show." I yawn again and climb out of the bed. I'm *starving*, so I walk downstairs and pray that Wendy left me something in the fridge.

Of course, she did, along with a note.

*Hey, kiddo:*

*You were sleeping like a baby, so I let you be. We'll catch up tomorrow, and you can tell me everything about the tour. Can't wait to hear about it! There's food in the fridge.*

*Xo,*

*Wendy*

I immediately pull out the big bowl of salad and pour some dressing over the top and dig in without dishing it into a bowl.

I live alone. I can do these things.

"Listen, I know you just got home after being away for months, but I was wondering if you'd consider a trip to Seattle."

I frown as I chew a big bite of kale and cucumber. "What's going on there? Is everything okay?"

"Well, I think we *finally* set a wedding date for later this summer. I know I've been so stupid about it, but my family is *big,* and there have been so many other weddings and stuff, you know?"

"Sure, but you deserve to have your wedding, too, Stella."

"Everyone keeps telling me that. Anyway, I'd love it if you could come and help me shop for a dress and do some fun wedding stuff with me. If you don't want to, or if you can't get away, I totally understand."

Actually, it's not a bad idea at all. Being in Nashville is only going to be a constant reminder that my career is in limbo. Maybe I need to get away and spend some time with people I love.

"You know what? I'm in."

"Really? Holy shit, thank you! I'm so excited! Now I just have to talk Maya into it, too. Your sister doesn't want to leave your parents for long these days."

"I'll talk her into coming for at least a couple of days," I assure Stella. "Don't worry about it. When do you want me there?"

"Whenever you can get here, honestly. I can work around your schedule."

"Let me get my bearings, and I'll keep you posted."

"Thanks, Sid. See you soon!"

And with that, she ends the call, and I'm left standing in my kitchen, eating salad out of a huge bowl in silence.

Without overthinking it, I open my laptop and, still eating this delicious salad, book a short-term vacation rental that just happens to be in the same building as my brother's condo.

Coincidence? Maybe, but I'm choosing to see it as a sign.

Tapping my phone, I call Wendy.

"Hi, Sid. How can I help?"

God, I love her.

"Hey, Wendy. I've decided to take a spur-of-the-moment trip…"

I DIDN'T TELL anyone that I was coming. I mean, Stella knew that I'd be in town at some point, but I didn't give anyone a heads-up.

Not even Gray.

And he's my best friend in the whole world.

But I wanted to surprise them. Surprises have always been my favorite thing, and I've been so busy for so long that I haven't been able to dole out the surprises often enough.

Now that I'm settled in the condo that's just four floors down from my brother's, I shoot him a text.

*Me: What are you up to this evening?*

The three little dots dance in the bubble on my screen as he replies.

*Gray: I'm just making some dinner with Stella. What are you up to? Recovered from the tour yet?*

I grin and don't even bother to grab my handbag. I'm not leaving the building. But I do make sure the door is securely locked behind me before heading to the elevator.

And when I reach Gray and Stella's door, I press the doorbell, bouncing on the balls of my feet in excitement.

The look on my brother's face, when he opens the door, does not disappoint.

"Surprise!"

"Holy shit." He tugs me inside and hugs me close, and then Stella runs my way and wraps her arms around both of us.

"You're here!" she exclaims. "Why didn't you tell us you were coming? I'll get the guest room ready."

"No need," I reply as I untangle myself from them. "I'm staying in a condo downstairs. Do you think I want to stay here and listen to you do the nasty all the time? Gross."

When I glance around, I realize that I'm not the only guest here tonight.

"I'm sorry. I didn't realize I was crashing a party."

"You're not crashing anything," Stella says with a laugh. "It's just dinner. You know Olivia and Vaughn, and I think you met Keaton, Liv's brother, at their wedding last year."

"Yeah." My eyes meet Keaton's, and that one night we spent together, the night of the wedding, comes flooding through my mind in full color. I managed to block out every sigh and every orgasm, but locking eyes with him now brings it all back.

And I wasn't ready for that.

"Hi, everyone," I say with a small wave, still watching Keaton. His green eyes haven't left mine, either. He just shoves his hands into his pockets and rocks back on his heels. His jaw clenches, and I can't help but wonder why I find that so sexy, but I do. His sharp jawline looks like it was carved out of stone. "Sorry to just barge in. I thought it would be fun to surprise these two."

"It *is* fun," Liv assures me. I know that Stella and Olivia have been best friends since infancy, as their mothers are also best friends. "And perfect timing because Stella and I were just about to boot the guys to the other room so we can look at dresses."

"Let's have dinner first," Stella declares and moves back into the kitchen.

"We're having salmon," Gray informs me. "And there's plenty, so don't worry."

He knows me so well.

"Cool. What can I do to help?"

"You can tell us everything about the tour," Liv says as she helps Stella toss a salad. "Was it as epic as it looked from our seats? Because it was one of the best shows I've ever seen."

"Coming from the niece of a rock legend, that's high praise," Gray adds with a wink.

I smile, delighted that they really seemed to enjoy the show, and then I take a deep breath. I'd rather not talk about work tonight.

"It was a good tour," I reply slowly. "Not the best one I've done, but I had a good time."

"I agree with Liv. We enjoyed it," Vaughn says with a wink. Vaughn Barrymore comes from Hollywood royalty and has starred in several movies for his father-in-law's production company. In fact, that's how he met Liv. She's one of the top costume designers for Williams Productions and had to work with Vaughn.

The rest is history.

"I'm so glad you enjoyed the show," I say, the way I always do whenever anyone compliments my concerts. "But let's not talk about it right now, okay? I'm on hiatus for a while."

That has my brother's head whipping around, and he narrows his eyes at me, but he doesn't ask the questions I can see burning in his eyes.

*What do you mean? You never take a hiatus. What happened?*

I shake my head a tiny bit, and he reads me loud and clear.

*Please don't ask me now. I'll tell you all about it later.*

The conversation turns to wedding plans for Stella

and Gray and new movies that are on deck for Vaughn, and the whole time, Keaton hasn't said a word.

But he sits next to me at the table.

And I can feel the heat from his arm as he reaches for the salt and pepper.

It makes my nether regions do the happy dance.

"So, how have you been, Keaton?" I ask before taking a bite of salmon.

"Fine."

I nod thoughtfully. "Boy, you don't let a girl get a word in edgewise, do you?"

Liv snorts at that. "He's a man of few words."

"What kind of cars have you been working on lately?" I ask him. I know that Keaton rebuilds expensive, hard-to-find vehicles and sells them to the highest bidder. Jay Leno has several of Keaton's cars in his huge garage.

"He's got a Mustang in his garage right now that Uncle Will has been salivating over," Stella informs me with a helpful smile. "Are you going to put the man out of his misery and sell it to him, Keat?"

"It's his," Keaton replies. "He might kill me in my sleep if I sold it to someone else."

Keaton goes quiet once more, and I'm surprised by how much that frustrates me. He may be on the quiet side around his family, but I remember very well that when he's naked and making me quiver in delight, he's *very* vocal.

*"That's right, baby, let go. Fucking come for me. God, you're gorgeous. Yes, just like that."*

I shiver, as if a chill has just run up my spine.

"You okay, Sid?" Gray asks.

"Sure. I'm probably just cold from the flight. Why are airplanes always so damn chilly?"

"Right?" Liv says, agreeing with me. "I always freeze my tits off on planes."

"I'll warm your tits up," Vaughn offers, making us all laugh.

"Of course, you will," Liv says and leans over to kiss her husband's lips. "That's so selfless of you."

"Dude." Keaton sits back and scowls at Vaughn. "That's my fucking sister."

# CHAPTER 2

## KEATON

*F*uck. Me.

The one woman in this universe that I can't get out of my head is sitting inches away from me, and everything in me wants to fuck her until she can't remember her own name.

I doubt her brother would appreciate it much if I did that on his own dining room table.

"I like the scruff." Sidney's voice is quiet as she picks at her salad. She hasn't eaten much of her dinner, but I chalk it up to her traveling most of the day. I know that my stomach doesn't settle for a while after flying.

When I don't answer her right away, she turns those baby blues up to stare at me.

"Are you just not speaking to me at all anymore? I thought we left things on better terms than that."

"No." I shake my head once, relieved that the others aren't paying any attention to us. They're too wrapped up in discussing the pros and cons of having a band versus a DJ for Gray and Stella's wedding. "That's not it. Sorry, I was surprised to see you. I'm not trying to be rude."

"Same goes," she says with a little sigh. The same kind of sigh that slipped through her lips when my fingers danced down her spine. "It's been a while. Almost a year?"

"About that," I agree, as Olivia breaks out in her rendition of beatboxing.

My sister is talented at a lot of things, but beatboxing isn't one of them.

"Don't quit your day job," I suggest and am met with her flipping me the bird, which just makes me grin.

"So, you're working on a Mustang, huh?" Sidney asks, obviously trying to make conversation. It's not that I don't want to talk to her. It's that my tongue always sticks to the roof of my mouth whenever I'm near her. She's the one woman in this world that both disarms me and makes me feel like a kid. I've done a good job my entire adult life of keeping women at arm's length.

Sidney's the only one I've been tempted to pull into my world.

And that can't happen.

Had I known that she'd be here tonight, I wouldn't have come. It's no one's fault. She wanted to surprise her brother and Stella, and I get that. It was fun for all of them.

28

But I'd give just about everything I own not to be here tonight, to avoid the awkwardness. Because Sidney and I can't happen.

"You're quiet again," she says with a resigned sigh.

I don't want to hurt her feelings, so I decide to suck it up. I might not want to be here, but I *am*, and I refuse to make Sid feel bad.

"It's been a long week," I lie easily and offer her a small smile.

"It's only Tuesday," she replies with a grin of her own.

"Isn't that a pisser?" That makes her laugh, and my stomach clenches into a tight ball. Everything about Sid is a one-two punch. Her laugh, her gorgeous blue eyes, and her body with curves for days have been the star of my dreams since I first met her at my sister's wedding last year.

Having her so close to me, knowing that I can't touch her or have her, is its own special form of torture.

But, with the goal of not hurting her feelings at the forefront of my mind, I laugh with her.

"It's okay," she continues as she finally takes a bite of her fish and follows it up with a sip of her cocktail. "I've had a crappy few months, so I get how it is."

"Why has it been a bad few months?" I suddenly want to hear everything she has to say.

She lifts her left shoulder, the one that's not

29

currently covered by fabric because her sweatshirt slid off and she left it exposed.

There's no bra strap, which tells me she's bare under that sweatshirt, and I remember exactly how her full breasts feel in my hands.

"Work." She takes another sip of her drink, looking around the table as if she's making sure they're all too caught up in their own conversation to listen in on ours. "The tour didn't do well. The album did worse. When I got home, my agent informed me that the label wasn't going to renew my contract."

The last few words are said in a whisper, and I have the intense, immediate desire to punch out the idiot who made the decision to let her go at the record company.

"I'm sorry, Sid." I reach under the table, where the others can't see, and pat her thigh. "They're idiots. The tour was awesome."

Her head whips around in surprise, and her eyes widen as she stares up at me. "How do you know?"

"I went with the others." I shrug as if it's no big deal.

"You were there, too?"

"Sure."

I glance down and see her swallow hard.

"I didn't know that," she says at last.

"I had a great time. You put on a hell of a show, so whoever the idiot is that decided to cut you loose is a first-rate moron."

That makes her smile again. "Thanks. It'll all work

out, and in the meantime, I have a break to rest and regroup, you know?"

"Sure. That makes sense."

"Keaton, you haven't even so much as sipped that drink," Stella says, frowning at me from across the table. "Did I make it wrong?"

"Oh, sorry." I pick up the highball glass and sip the old-fashioned that Stella made for me. She knows it's my favorite. "That hits the spot, Stell."

"If you don't like it, I can remake it."

"Nope, it's great. Dinner's good, too."

"I brought a chocolate cake for dessert," Olivia announces to us all. "Because I've been craving chocolate like crazy."

"I'll never turn that down," Sidney replies. "When do we get to talk about wedding dresses?"

"Now," Stella decides as she stands and clears her plate from the table. Liv and Sidney join her, and they quickly cut three big pieces of cake before they hustle out of the room and down the hall, where the menfolk can't eavesdrop.

Not that we want to.

"We forgot the drinks," Liv announces as she comes running back into the room. She bypasses the dining room, heads for the kitchen, then runs back the way she came, carrying a shaker full of fresh cocktails. "See you later!"

"Stella's been excited about this all day," Gray says

as he stands and begins to clear the other dishes from the table.

Vaughn and I follow suit, helping him with the dishes.

"She's finally getting excited about the wedding thing," Vaughn says. "She texts or calls Liv about it all the time."

Gray nods as he opens the dishwasher. "I don't think it was that she *wasn't* amped up about the wedding before. There's just been a lot going on with the family lately, with other engagements, weddings, and football games thrown in."

"It's been a busy year," I agree and sip my drink. "But we all want Stella to have the wedding she wants. She shouldn't have to feel like she has to put it off just because we have a busy family. That's never going to change."

"I finally convinced her of that," Gray says with a nod. "So, we're moving forward with it. The way things are going, there might just be more than one wedding a year for a while, given how big the Montgomery and Williams family is."

"They're all dropping like flies," Vaughn agrees, then turns to me with a half smile.

"Why are you looking at me like that?"

"You just might be one of those flies."

I shake my head and let out a laugh. "That's ridiculous. I don't plan to get married, man."

"*Ever?*" Gray's face registers surprise.

"Ever. It's not for me. I just don't trust people, you know?"

"I get it." Vaughn pats my shoulder, then rubs his hand down his face, his wedding ring glinting in the light of the kitchen. "Trust is hard under normal circumstances. Throw in the extraordinary life that you live, and the people you're related to, and I know that it's almost impossible. I come from the same kind of family. Mine isn't as close, and it definitely isn't as big, but it is just as famous."

"Yeah, I know you get it. I have a small circle," I confirm. "And I'm not mad about it. But no, marriage isn't for me."

"You're no virgin," Gray says.

"Fuck no." I laugh again and reach for my drink. "I'm not a monk. But the women I choose to be with know the score. No surprises, no hurt feelings."

"Aren't you the romantic one," Vaughn says with a wink, and I just shake my head.

"I'll romance the cars I fix up. That's about all the romance I need."

Gray opens his mouth to reply, but before he can, the girls come tumbling back into the room. They're giggling and a little sloppier than they were before.

The cocktails are doing their job.

"I like the black one," Liv announces, clearly being funny. "Black with big, poofy sleeves."

"I prefer the red," Sidney replies. "The one that's

see-through. You have excellent nipples to pull that one off."

"I know you're kidding," Gray says calmly as he wraps his arm around Stella's waist and leans in to kiss her cheek.

"You *don't* want to see my nipples?" Stella asks him, then sticks her lower lip out in a pout.

"Not when you walk down the aisle."

"Uncle Nate would be quite scandalized," Liv reminds everyone, and I can't help but scowl at the thought.

"He'd kill someone," I put in. "*Anyone.* And then he'd wrap you from head to toe in a weighted blanket to make sure you're covered up."

"Probably not worth it," Stella decides. "Hey, thanks for doing the dishes."

"You cooked," Gray says with a shrug and then notices as his sister succumbs to a huge yawn. "You're probably beat, huh?"

"Me? Nah." Sid shakes her head, but her eyes are heavy. "I can party all night. Hell, on concert night, I'd barely be through the first three songs by now."

"It's not concert night," Liv reminds her. "You're staying downstairs in this building?"

"Yeah, I found a short-term rental just a few floors down. I thought it was convenient. But you're probably right, I should go to bed."

"You should walk her down," Stella says to me.

"She's had a lot to drink. Make sure she gets there all right."

"Oh, he doesn't have to—"

"I was going to head out anyway," I cut in, pushing off the stool in front of the kitchen island. "I'll walk you down."

"I'm so glad you're here," Stella says as she hugs Sidney and kisses her cheek. "I'll take tomorrow off of work so I can hang with you."

"You *really* don't have to do that," Sidney insists, but Stella's shaking her head.

"Trust me, I could use a day off."

There are hugs all around, and then I'm suddenly alone with Sidney in the hallway, walking down to the elevator.

"I'm sure I'll make it to my rental just fine," she says as she steps into the elevator.

"I know you will because I'll make sure of it."

I step inside, and the doors slide shut, and I glance over at her. Her eyes are heavy-lidded from the alcohol, but she's steady on her feet.

"Ever since I read *Fifty Shades of Grey* back in the day, I've always had a thing for sexy times in elevators," she says.

But before I can pin her to the wall and kiss her, the doors open again, and she walks out ahead of me.

"I'm in four-oh-six."

"Gray's nine-oh-six."

"Yep." She grins as she approaches her door. "I'm

35

right below him. But not *right* below him. Maybe I drank more than I thought."

"You're tired."

I wait while she keys in the code to the door, and when it opens, I take a step back.

"Have a good time in Seattle, Sid."

Before I can head back down to the elevator, she slips her hand in mine, and I turn back to her, one eyebrow raised.

"What if there's a monster in the condo?"

"I'm no monster slayer."

Her lips twitch. "Get in here."

# CHAPTER 3

## SIDNEY

"*I* don't believe that you're afraid of anything." Keaton follows me into the condo, closes the door behind him, and waits while I turn on some lights. His eyebrows climb when the space is illuminated. "This doesn't look anything like Gray's place."

I grin and quickly scan the room. Gray's condo is modern, with clean lines and little pops of color here and there.

This one looks like Joanna Gaines on steroids.

While the two condos have identical floor plans, they are definitely not the same.

"Whoever owns this place really loves the farmhouse look," I agree with a laugh. "There's a *Live, Laugh, Love* sign in every room."

"Interesting." He's walking slowly around the room

as if he's trying to stay away from me, and I'm not too proud to admit that it stings a little.

The last time I saw him, he couldn't keep his hands to himself and had me naked in less than four seconds, panting and moaning in three minutes, and I believe I had that first orgasm at the speed of light.

Now, you'd think I have a communicable disease.

"Don't look at me like that." His voice is low, his hands tight in fists as he shakes his head and continues slowly stalking around the outer edge of the room.

"Like what?"

"Like you're a lion and I'm a gazelle."

I can't help but snort at that. "I mean, you're lean, but you're no gazelle."

He doesn't laugh. He doesn't even crack a smile.

"Okay, listen." I swallow hard and look down at my hands. "You got me home safely. If you don't want to stay, you certainly don't have to. I didn't mean to make you feel uncomfortable."

I march over to the front door, my pleasant buzz from earlier long gone, and reach for the knob, but before I can turn it, I'm spun around and am staring into the greenest eyes I've ever seen.

"It's not that I don't want to be here, damnit."

"Okay. What is it, then?"

I lift my chin, almost defiantly, as he stares down at me, breathing a little hard, looking more than a little intense. Jesus, he's so fucking *sexy*. His dark hair is longer than I remember it being before and begs for my fingers to run through it. He has that hot-as-hell scruff on his face, and his eyes...my god, those eyes. I could get lost in those cool green pools.

I *have* gotten lost in them.

Every time I'm near him, my body has a visceral reaction, as if I've known him forever. As if I were made for everything and anything he could possibly do to me.

"You won't hurt my feelings if you go," I say into the silence.

Sure, it's a lie.

But I'll be damned if I'll beg for him to want me. Not even Keaton Williams is worth that kind of humiliation.

"I shouldn't want you so fucking bad."

I don't reply as relief floods me. He *does* want me. But I don't reach for him because something tells me that it wouldn't be welcome right now. I wait and watch with fascination as it looks like he's waging an internal war against himself, emotions I can't even name flooding across his face.

Finally, his face clears, as if he's made a decision.

"So, see you later?"

But he doesn't leave. He cups my face, touching me for the first time since we came into the condo, and kisses me like *he's* the lion. Like he's starving for me, and all the doubts I had over the past ten minutes are gone.

My hands dive into his hair as his slide down my

39

torso and around to cup my ass. He lifts me easily into his arms, carrying me through the condo.

"Which bedroom?"

"The big one," I reply with a grin before burying my face in his neck and biting him there.

I can't help it. I'm a biter.

In a matter of seconds, I'm flat on my back on the bed, and Keaton's standing over me, chest heaving, as he reaches over his shoulder and tugs his shirt off in that really sexy way that men do. When he's bare from the waist up, I begin to salivate.

"Jesus, how did you get *more* abs?"

His lips twitch as he pops the button on his jeans, but I quickly scoot over to him and bat his hands away.

"I got this."

He doesn't argue. His fingers comb through my loose hair as I unzip his jeans and then push them over his hips and down his legs.

Keaton steps out of them and kicks them aside.

"You're not wearing underwear."

"No, ma'am."

I've never considered dicks to be…*attractive*. I know that men are proud of them, but they're not exactly pretty.

Unless you're Keaton Williams.

He's already hard as stone, and all I have to do is lean in just a few inches to take him into my mouth.

"Fucking hell," he groans.

I push down until he's touching the back of my throat before pulling up once again, my lips tight around him.

And before I can do any more, Keaton takes my shoulders in his hands and pushes me back to the mattress.

"Hey!"

"Can't." His voice is like gravel now as he kisses my neck and my chest, pulling my sweatshirt out of his way. "I want you too much. I won't last, Sid."

His hands are urgent and possessive as he works to get me naked, which doesn't take long because I'm not wearing any underwear either.

Not even a bra.

I thought I was going to spend a casual evening with Gray and Stella.

"Fuck, babe." He brushes the tip of his nose over my already hard nipple. "You're even better than I remember, and that's saying something because I remember you being *perfect.*"

I grin up at him. "You're just being charming."

"No." He watches my face as his fingers dance down my belly, over my navel, and then farther south to the promised land. "You're the most beautiful thing I've ever seen in my life."

I gasp when his fingers push inside of me, and when the pad of his thumb covers my clit, my back arches off the bed, and I cry out as electricity shoots through me.

"Fuck!"

"Yes, baby. That's right." He knows just how to move those fingers, how to bend and slide to hit just the right spots. "God, you're beautiful when you come."

I can't speak. I can only feel as wave after wave rolls through me.

And when I can take a whole breath once again, I realize that he's kissing my stomach and my hip. His fingers haven't left me, but they've slowed down, as if he's just lazily petting the inside of me.

It's damn nice.

"I don't have any condoms." Is that *my* voice? All breathless and full of need. "I didn't think—"

"I got it." He dives over the side of the bed and comes back with one single condom.

"Wallet?" I ask, and he just grins as he bites the foil and tears it open. "If we only have one of those, we'd better take our time."

"You're gonna kill me dead if you even think about asking me to wait."

I laugh as he rolls on the condom, and then I sit up and reverse our positions. He's lying beneath me, those green eyes on fire as he watches me rise up and slowly take him inside of me.

His eyes roll back into his head for the briefest moment, and then his hands are on my ass, and I'm slowly moving up and down, loving every inch of him.

My hands are braced on his chest, but he easily sits up, takes my hands and kisses them, then loops them around his neck as I do the same with my legs around his waist, and I'm no longer controlling the tempo.

I'm not mad about it.

I remember that Keaton likes to be in control in bed, and it's damn thrilling. I don't have to *think;* I don't have to be in charge of anything the way I am in my everyday life.

I can just *feel* when I'm with him.

And he takes care of the rest.

"Oh, shit, I'm close." I tip my forehead against his, breathing him in.

"Let go," he coaxes. His voice is gentle, and with one hand still planted on my backside, he reaches up with the other and brushes his fingertips down my cheek, then circles around my throat, not squeezing, not hurting me, just taking charge. "Come on, beautiful, let go for me."

I couldn't resist him if I tried. Everything in me shatters. My core tightens around him, and my breath comes out in shudders.

And he absorbs all of it, not succumbing to his own orgasm until I'm just on the other side of mine.

"Christ," he mutters, still watching me with those intense eyes. His hands tighten, but he's still careful not to hurt me. And when we're both on the other side, panting and sweating and a tangle of loose limbs, I lean in to hug him close.

He kisses my shoulder.

I don't want to move.

I don't want it to be over yet. Will he leave like he did the last time? I'd rather he stay.

And that's not normal for me.

"Don't go," I whisper before he moves to untangle us. "Stay with me tonight."

He's quiet for a moment and then kisses my shoulder again. "Let me go for a minute."

He easily lifts me off him, and as I roll to the side, he gets up from the bed and pads into the bathroom.

The door is closed, with the light seeping through along the floor, giving me enough light to walk through the room to the other bathroom in the condo so I can clean myself up. On the way back to the bedroom, I make a pit stop at the closet so I can put on a tank and another pair of leggings.

When I return to the bedroom, I'm surprised to find Keaton has turned on the bedside light and climbed under the covers of the bed, still naked.

He's not getting dressed.

"You're staying?" I can hear the surprise in my voice.

"You asked me to." He looks uncertain now, and I race over, jump into the bed, and snuggle up to him.

"I didn't think you would. But I'm glad you are. Unless you don't want to."

"Stop talking." With his finger under my chin, he lifts my face to his and kisses me firmly. "I want to stay. Thanks for the invite."

I grin up at him before I nuzzle his chest. He

reaches over and turns out the light, and we're cast into darkness, with the glow of the lights of the city.

"How long will you be in Seattle?" he asks softly.

"I don't have a return ticket." His hands tighten on my back. "For the first time in a *really* long time, I don't have a plan."

"Is that unnerving?"

"Oh, yeah, it is." I look up at him, enjoying the way the gray light is cast on his face. "Maybe we can just enjoy each other while I'm here."

Keaton licks his lips. "I'd like that, but, Sid, I don't want to lead you on. I like you a lot, and the sex is fucking incredible, but that's all it can be."

I have so many questions. I want to drill him, ask *why* he feels that way, but for now, I just nod.

"I respect that and appreciate your honesty. Friends with benefits, while I'm in town, works for me. But I have one condition."

He turns wary eyes to mine. "Okay, what is it?"

"While you're fucking me, you're not fucking anyone else. And vice versa, of course."

He moves quickly, pinning me beneath him on the bed, and kisses me long and slow. When he pulls back, he smiles softly down at me. "There is no one else I want, Sid. There's no one."

"Okay, then. It's decided. We'd better stock up on condoms."

I NEED A PIANO.

I can play guitar, as well, but I like to write on the piano, and there isn't one here in this condo.

I'll send the owner an email today to ask if they have any objections to me having one brought in. I can lease one while I'm in town.

I woke early, before Keaton, and silently slipped from the bed. Now, I'm sitting on the couch, with my second cup of coffee, watching the city wake up.

Feeling movement to my left, I glance over and see Keaton standing in the doorway, wearing only his jeans, which aren't done up all the way and hang loosely on his impressive hips, showing off those abs.

"Coffee," is all he says.

"There's a fresh pot in the kitchen."

He nods and pads over, pours himself a mug, and then joins me on the couch.

"I can see why my brother likes living in this building so much." I take a sip of coffee and glance back out the windows. "Even though we grew up in a tiny town, Gray's always been a city boy. He would love being in the heart of all the action."

"Do you miss Coeur d' Alene?"

I shrug a shoulder and glance his way. He's watching me with those sleepy eyes.

"Sure, I do. I miss my parents. Mom's been doing better now that she's on the right medication."

"Dementia is a bitch."

I nod and frown down into my mug. "I have a lot of guilt. Maya's the one who's taken on the load of making sure that Mom has everything she needs. She left her job in Spokane so she could move in with them."

"From what I hear, she didn't mind doing those things."

"No, she didn't. But still. Gray's in Seattle, and I'm... well, I'm *everywhere*. I hate that she shoulders that burden alone. Before I go back to Nashville, I'll make a trip over to see them."

He's quiet for a long moment, and it's nice. We're just drinking our coffee, soaking in the morning.

"I have to find a piano today. I have a melody playing in my head, and I want to tinker with it. What are you up to?"

"Work." He sips his coffee. "Always work."

"We're a couple of workaholics." I grin over at him. "Thanks for staying last night."

"It wasn't a hardship."

That makes me laugh. "I'm so happy to hear that."

"I'm going to leave after this cup."

"I figured."

He sighs and pushes his hand through his messy hair.

"I don't have your number." He looks surprised, as if the thought just occurred to him.

I grab my phone and open an empty text. "What's yours?"

He rattles it off, and I plug it in, then send a simple text to him and hit send.

We hear a ping in the bedroom.

"There, now you have it."

"Cool. I'll be in touch."

"I'll be around."

# CHAPTER 4

## KEATON

"*D*ude, you should have won that game," my cousin, Liam, says to Ike as they idly toss a football back and forth in my garage, where I'm currently buried in the business end of the engine of this classic Mustang.

"I can only do my part, man," Ike replies.

Ike Harrison is the newest member of our clan, recently married to my cousin Sophie, who happens to be Liam's older sister. Ike is also the star quarterback for Seattle's professional football team, and given that our uncle is Will Montgomery, a football legend, the men in this family can discuss the sport ad nauseam.

Including me.

"Your defensive line coach was slacking," Drew adds, and I pull myself out of the car long enough to take in the scene.

Drew is yet another cousin, and all three men

decided that today was the day to show up at my garage to hang out and chat. It happens often, cousins or aunts and uncles popping in to see what I'm working on and to spend time with me.

It doesn't bother me at all.

But I can't let these guys know that, or they'll be here every day, and this will be their new hangout.

"If you'd like to have a football meeting, you can do that somewhere else." I reach for a socket wrench but discover that my hand is covered in grease, so I pull the rag out of my back pocket to wipe it off first.

"Why are you pissy today?" Liam scowls over at me. "You're always the even-keeled one of the group."

"I'm not pissy. I'm *busy.*"

Ike throws the ball to me, and I easily drop the rag and catch it.

"I can't just play catch all day. I have to get this Mustang finished so I can work on the next project."

"What *is* the next project?" Drew walks around the car, examining it as if it was on a lot and he was in the market for it.

"If you kick the tires, I'll kick *you.*"

"Yep, pissy," Ike says with a toothy grin. "Want me to have Sophie come over and cheer you up?"

Soph and I are close. Out of all the cousins, she's probably the one that I confide in the most, the one I've always felt the closest connection with. And her husband knows that.

Hell, everyone knows that.

"It might be a job for my sister," Liam says, nodding. "I'll call her."

"Don't call her. I'm fine. I'm just on a roll with work, and you three stooges showed up to interrupt me."

"I'm not a stooge," Drew says. "Answer the question. What's the next project?"

I usually have three going at any given time. One that I'm finishing up on, one that I'm hip-deep into, and one that I have my sights on and can't wait to start.

"Don't laugh," I say with a sigh, resigned to them doing just that as I stalk over to the fridge and pull out a bottle of water, taking a long pull. "It's a 1983 Jeep Wagoneer."

All three of them just blink at me. No, it's not a sexy sports car or even a super-old classic that's hard to find.

"A *station wagon*?" Liam asks, his brows drawn together. "Like, a huge family car from the olden days?"

"Yeah." I shrug, drink the rest of the bottle, and chuck it into the recycling bin. "It's a commissioned piece. These old Wagoneers are popular right now. They're nostalgic."

"Hey, you do what you have to do," Ike says. "We all have to make a living."

We're silent for a minute, and then we bust up laughing. Sure, I do it to make a living, but I don't *need* it. I love it. Pure and simple.

"You didn't make fun of me when I was restoring my '73 Bronco."

"That's a *Bronco*," Drew says, as if that explains everything. "It's fun. It's masculine and cool."

"Point taken." I reach for the socket wrench. "When does practice start for the new season, Ike?"

"We never really stop training, but we don't start getting ready for the season until mid-summer. So, a couple more months. I was thinking about taking Sophie somewhere for a few days. What do you guys think? Maybe Hawaii?"

"She loves Hawaii," I reply. "I think someone in the family has a house on the beach in Maui. Who is that?"

"My mom and dad," Drew confirms. "They'll let you use it, no problem."

"That's awesome, and it's pretty damn convenient being part of this family because, I swear, y'all own homes pretty much everywhere in the world, but I want to take her to a spa. Let her get pampered and polished. Maybe shop some."

"You're pretty much speaking the love language of every woman in this family," Liam says with a laugh. "That'll get you laid. Do it. Wait, did you fuck up and this is how you're trying to get back on her good side?"

"No, I didn't fuck up. I'm just trying to be nice to my wife. So I *stay* on her good side."

"Good plan." I nod, pleased that one of my favorite people has found such a good guy. "Will you still be around for the big party at Aunt Sam and Uncle Leo's place next weekend?"

"Yeah. I figure we'll leave after that. It's too fun to miss."

"I think it's the one thing every year that the whole family makes sure they're in town for," I agree. I glance longingly at the car that isn't finished and that I didn't get enough done on today. "I have to lock up and go."

"It's Sunday," Drew says. "Where do you have to be?"

"Dinner at my parents' place. It's Haley's birthday. And, yeah, we'll be celebrating all this month's birthdays at Sam and Leo's party, but Mom insists that we still do a little party with the immediate family. So, I'm going over there. She's turning twenty-four this week."

"We don't have any cousins under eighteen anymore, since Emma and Finn both just turned eighteen," Drew replies. "Crazy, huh?"

"I think Uncle Dom might lock Emma in a tower at the vineyard. She's gorgeous, and he's a little overprotective."

"We all are," I remind Liam. "Now, get the hell out of my garage so I'm not late. Haley will never let me forget it if I show up late to her birthday party."

"Tell them all hi," Drew says as the three of them walk out ahead of me, and I lock up behind us. "See you next weekend."

"See you."

They all pile into Ike's new Toyota 4Runner. Because he has a nationwide endorsement contract with the auto company, he gets a new vehicle yearly. I offered to find him a classic 4Runner and restore it for him, but he passed. Said it would be a waste because he's supposed to drive around in the new one.

Ike honks the horn and waves his hand out the window as they drive down my driveway toward the main road.

My house is bigger than necessary, but I wanted this shop. It has all the space I need to have up to three projects going at a time, which is about all I can handle by myself.

My dad suggested that I hire help so I can turn out more projects, but for now, I rejected the idea. I have subcontractors I use for the parts that I can't do myself, and I do the rest. It could be pride, or it could be ego.

Mostly, it feels like therapy.

The drive to my parents' place doesn't take long. I key my way through the gate and then drive up to the house. I see that Haley's already here. She's been living at the Cousin Compound, as we call it, for a while now, and she loves it. Most of us grew up in chaotic households, so to have the compound available to all the cousins, for as long as they need it, is pretty great.

I couldn't do it. I like my solitude, my alone time. But I know that I'm the odd man out when it comes to that opinion.

As soon as I walk into the house that my parents have owned since long before I was born, I feel like I'm home. Sure, Mom's changed things over the years, but it's still home.

"You're here," Mom says with that happy smile she always has whenever her kids come home. "Liv and Vaughn should be here any minute. We're going to eat in the outdoor kitchen. Here, take these plates out."

She kisses my cheek before she passes me two heaping plates of appetizers, and I follow orders, heading outside where Dad's manning the grill and Haley and Chelsea are arguing over...well, I have no idea what they're bickering about.

"Mom sent me out here with these." I set the plates on the table and smile at Haley. "Happy Birthday, kiddo."

"Thanks. Where's my present?"

"Maybe I didn't get you one."

She just watches me with cool blue eyes, just like our father's, and waits.

Finally, I pull a box out of my back pocket and pass it over. It's blue with a white bow and comes from her favorite store.

"Oh my gosh, you *shouldn't* have!"

I roll my eyes and walk over to Dad. "Those burgers smell good."

He grins, then gestures with his chin to where Haley and Chelsea are oohing and aahing over the silver earrings I got her. "Good job there."

"The girls in this family are too easy. Just buy jewelry that comes in the blue box, and everyone is happy."

He laughs and pats my shoulder before returning to

the grill. "Just so you know, this half is beef, and this half is…plant-based."

I wrinkle my nose at him. "What?"

"Don't make fun of my impossible burgers," Haley calls out. "They're better for you than red meat. You should try them."

"Sure. As soon as the sun sets in the east and pigs fly out of my ass."

She just rolls her eyes and fastens the second earring to her ear.

"Gotta keep the girls happy," is all that Dad says as he lowers the lid on the grill so the burgers can cook. For as long as I can remember, it's been Dad's mission in life to keep the women in his life happy. He could give a flying fuck about Hollywood, but the family? He'd die for any of us. "What did you do today?"

"Worked. A few of the guys came over to hang out for a while."

"It's good that they can come to the garage and hang out with you."

"Except they drive me nuts and make it hard to get anything done." I just smile and accept the beer he offers me. "But it's all good. What did you do today?"

"Your mother had me working in the garden," he replies with a bright smile.

"You hate gardening."

"Yes, I do."

"Then why are you smiling like that?"

"Because your mother was with me, and she was hot as hell."

"I'm going to need more than one beer for this conversation."

Dad just laughs as the door opens and out walks Olivia and Vaughn, followed closely by Mom.

"Look who I found," Mom says with a laugh as Dad pulls her into his arms and lays a big, disgusting kiss on her.

"You need to warn me before you do that." I back away at the sound of their laughter and join my siblings and Vaughn at the table. "Why aren't you opening that?"

I gesture to the present Liv just sat in the middle of the table and Haley shrugs. "Because she told me I couldn't."

"You didn't give me a choice."

Haley just grins, and I shake my head.

"Sisters are a pain in the ass."

"Hey!" all three of them object at once, making Vaughn and I laugh.

"Oh, Keat, you're going out with some of us on Wednesday," Liv informs me as she munches on some fried zucchini.

"No, I'm not."

"Yes," she insists, "you are. It's a date thing. I'm setting you up."

"Absolutely not." Images of Sidney immediately take up residence in my head, of her smile and her laugh and her naked and writhing beneath me. I'm not seeing anyone else.

Not that my family knows that.

"Come *on*," Liv says, frowning over at me. "It's going to be fun. We're all coupled up, and I want you to go with this one person."

"Who is it?" Chelsea wants to know.

"I'm not telling," Liv says, shaking her head. "It's a blind date."

"It better not be one of Vaughn's famous friends or some actress you've been making costumes for, Liv. You know I don't date famous people."

"Hey, I'm an innocent bystander," Vaughn says, holding his hands up in surrender.

"You really need to get over that," Liv says before popping a piece of broccoli into her mouth. "Not all famous people are the same as that has-been that was a jerk to you in high school."

"I don't have to get over anything. Listen, I don't like being set up, and I'm just not interested in the whole thing."

"Oh, come on," Mom chimes in. "I think it's a great idea. You need to get out there and date more, honey."

"No, I don't."

Dad winks at me, but I notice that he's also not helping me out here.

"It'll be so much *fun*," Liv insists, bouncing up and down in her seat now. "I promise. I wouldn't steer you wrong or try to hook you up with someone who isn't *awesome.*"

"I'm not hooking up with anyone."

Aside from Sid, that is. In fact, I plan to go to her place when I leave here. I've been at her place every night this week.

"Don't be an idiot," Haley says, rolling her eyes. "You don't have to *hook up* with every single date you go on. It's just a fun night out."

"If it sounds so fun to you, *you* go with them."

"I already have plans." Haley's grin is toothy and full of sarcasm. She's such a brat.

"I really think that you should go," Mom adds again as Dad opens the top of the grill to pull off the finished patties. "It sounds like fun to me, and you just don't go out enough."

"How do you know?"

"A mother knows," is all she says, in that mysterious way she does. And the kicker is, she *does* always know.

How does she do that?

"Fine." I close my eyes and wonder what I've gotten myself into. "Fine. If it'll make you all shut up about it, I'll go. But I won't promise to like it or to like this person you're setting me up with. I can't believe I agreed to this."

"Well, you did, and no take backs," Liv declares. "It's going to be *awesome.* Soph and Ike are coming, and a bunch of other people you like. It won't be painful. I promise."

"Right. Sure. Whatever you say."

I stare at Vaughn, but he just shrugs.

"I just do what I'm told, man."

"Good idea," my dad says as he sets a big plate of burgers on the table. "This side is beef. That side is… something else. Eat at your own risk."

~

I CAN HEAR the piano playing as I walk down the hallway to Sidney's condo. I wonder if her neighbors can hear her, and if so, is she driving them crazy?

Sid texted me earlier and told me that the door was unlocked, but I still rap my knuckles on it twice before pushing inside.

She's sitting at the piano she rented earlier this week, bent over the keys, wrapped up in whatever she's playing. I don't recognize the song as one of hers.

Maybe it's the new one she mentioned that's been going through her mind lately.

It's a ballad, and it's pretty, whatever it is.

Rather than interrupt her, I sit on the couch behind her and listen. Her hands move over the keys as if they're stroking a long-time lover. As she builds to the bridge, she tips her chin up and arches her back into the music, the same way she does when we're having sex and she's about to come.

It's no less intriguing and sexy now than it is then.

She hasn't played for me before. We're always too

wrapped up in other things, too wrapped up in each other, to take the time for it.

And now that I'm sitting here listening, it occurs to me that I should ask her to play for me more often. Not because I'm seeking a private concert from the ultra-famous Sidney Sterling.

No, it's because this woman that I've grown to like so much is talented, and being alone with her as she makes music is one of the most intimate moments we've shared.

And she doesn't even know it yet.

When she finishes the song, I softly clap, and she turns on the bench to smile at me.

"I knew you were there."

"I didn't want to interrupt. I wanted to listen."

"I figured. That's the melody that's been chasing me down for a while."

"It's beautiful. Does it have words yet?"

"A few," is all she says as she watches me. "How's the family?"

"They're all fine. Haley had a good birthday. She talked me into taking a bite of something called an impossible burger, and I was pretty sure I was about to die."

"I've heard of those. I figure, if you're going to have a burger, have a *burger*."

"That's what I'm saying." I grin at her, and she returns it with one of her own. "Your eyes are so gorgeously blue."

"And here I was just thinking about how damn green yours are, and how it should be illegal for them to look that damn good."

She knocks me off balance with comments like that. They're not practiced or fake. She just says what she's thinking, and it's surprisingly refreshing.

"Maybe later you can play the piano for me without any clothes on."

"The bench might be cold," she says with a laugh.

"Don't worry, you can sit on my lap."

# CHAPTER 5

The way he looks at me makes me want to shiver in anticipation. He's such an intense man, so serious most of the time. There's not a goofy bone in his body, at least not one that I've seen yet. And that, surprisingly, doesn't bother me at all because when he does give me one of his disarming smiles, it's like the best gift in the world.

When Keaton smiles, you know that he means it. There's no pretense with this man at all, and that's awesome.

I hate guessing games.

"You're awfully far away."

And there's the smile that I've grown to love in such a short time. Not a huge, toothy smile, but a smug one that tugs his lips up in the corners, as if he's amused by me.

Which is good because I'm amused by me, too.

"What would you like me to do about that?" he asks and leans forward, planting his elbows on his knees.

"I'd like you to come over here."

He doesn't hesitate. He stands and walks to me, lifts me off the piano bench, then sits, and I straddle his lap.

"Now what?" he asks.

"Kiss me."

"No problem." He brushes my hair back as he braces my face in his hands and presses his lips to mine. Our tongues dance as I sink into him and wrap my arms around his neck. I can't help but grind my center against his denim-covered cock.

I *always* want him. When he's nearby, my body yearns for him, and he must feel the same way because we're rarely clothed when we're together.

"Bedroom," I say against his lips, but he doesn't move away from the piano. Instead, he lifts me on top of it and sets me down. The keys tinkle as my feet rest on them, and I watch with fascination as, in front of these open windows, Keaton pulls my loose shirt over my head and lets it fall to the floor.

He doesn't bother to work my pajama pants down. Instead, he just rips the crotch of them, and I can't help but laugh.

"Impatient much?"

"Always, when it comes to you." His voice is rougher now, his hands a little more demanding as they rub up and down my now-bare thighs. He's spread me open, but his eyes aren't pinned to my center in the soft glow of the nearby lamp.

They're on mine, watching my every reaction to his touch, to his voice.

I bite my lip and tip my head back as his fingers find my already wet center, but he leans in and plants his lips on that sweet spot just below my ear.

"Eyes on me, baby."

Complying, I open my heavy eyelids and see that his face has softened, his eyes full of humor and affection as his fingers play me as expertly as I did this piano just a few minutes ago.

"How do you know me so well?" I didn't mean to voice the question out loud, and before I can take it back, he grins once more.

"I've been studying you," he says. "Watching what you like. What makes you moan or clench or move."

"I think that just about everything you do makes me crazy."

He kisses me again, working me into a frenzy with those talented hands.

"Want you," I whisper against his lips, "inside of me."

Reaching for his jeans, I pull the button free, and the zipper opens. He's hard and falls out into my hand, and I relish the heavy feel of him against my skin.

I expect a flurry of hands and clothes and impatience, but he stays steady, slowly removing his clothes while watching me.

And when I pull up on his cock and brush my thumb over the head, he clenches his jaw.

"Are we really going to do this on a piano?" I ask him. "I mean, you're tall, but this doesn't look easy to me."

"Nothing about you is *easy*," he replies as he pulls a condom out of his jeans. "I don't want easy."

"You know what I mean."

He grips my thighs in his hands and pulls me forward until my ass is hanging off the piano, and with his strong hands supporting me, braced on my backside, he slides into me.

He's tall *and* strong, which means that while this looks awkward to me, it's easy for him.

And because he's Keaton, he takes charge, knowing exactly what I need and how to get it for me.

It's like he can read my damn mind.

When he slides inside of me, I can't help but close my eyes.

"Eyes." He kisses my chest. "On. Me."

God, I love it when he gets bossy in the bedroom.

Or, in this case, on the piano.

"I need to see your eyes," he says and begins to set a hard, fast pace, fucking me on this piano as if he does it every day.

With our eyes locked, he sends me into another world, full of light and color and heat and *every* feeling all at once. I can hear myself moaning, calling out for him, and I reach out to grip on to his arms as he increases the pace. The keys bang with every thrust, adding the pounding notes to the air, mixing with our grunts and moans.

Finally, he pushes us both over the edge into oblivion.

Before I can fall over the edge of the piano, he lifts me into his arms and walks me to the couch, where he sits and cradles me on his lap as we both work to catch our breath.

"I won't disclose to the rental company that I had *really* good sex on their piano."

"We might have to buy it, just for sentimental reasons."

I grin and lay my cheek on his chest, and when his arms come around me and squeeze me against him, I let out a long sigh.

"You okay?" he asks.

"I'm still humming from that last orgasm. Of course, I'm okay."

"That's good to hear, but I don't mean that. You looked kind of sad while you were playing when I got here."

"You could only see the back of my head."

I shift so I can look up at him, and he brushes a piece of hair off my cheek and kisses my forehead.

"Chalk it up to body language, then. If you don't want to talk about it, that's cool, too."

"I don't think *sad* is the right word," I admit, thinking it over. I reach over for a throw blanket and wrap it around us to keep the chill off. "I guess I have moments when I wonder if my career is over. I'm in my mid-twenties, and I might be all dried up when it comes to country music, and the thought of that makes me very sad. So, maybe you're right, and sad *was* the right word after all."

"Do you really believe that Nashville is done with you?"

I frown at the prick of tears behind my eyes. When he puts it that way, yeah, it rips my heart out of my chest.

"God, I hope not."

"Maybe this is just the universe's way of telling you that you needed to rest. Spend some time in Seattle and have a mutually satisfying adult relationship with a hot guy who rocks your world every chance he gets."

"Who says I don't have that in Nashville?"

He goes very still, and when I tip my head back once more to look at him, his eyes have gone hard.

"I don't," I add, and cup his face gently in my hand. "For the record, I'm as single as they come."

"Good, because I don't poach."

"You're much too good of a human to do that."

He smirks, but I shake my head and straddle him, bracing my hands on the back of the sofa on either side of his head. "It's true. I may not know you inside and out, but I'm a good judge of character, and I know, deep down, that you're not a prick who doesn't care what the relationship status of a girl is before you sleep with her."

"My parents raised me better than that," he admits with a small shrug. "Hell, I come from a huge family of *very* monogamous people. It's almost disgusting how in love they all are. Just today, my dad made a point of telling me how hot he thinks my mom is."

"I think that's sweet."

"It's not your parents."

I laugh and lean into him again. "My parents are the same way. They never held back on showing affection for each other around us kids. They've always been totally devoted to each other. I think that's why it's been so hard to watch my dad have to cope with my mom's illness."

"Maybe that's one other thing that makes you a little sad."

I nod but don't look up at him.

"Are you hungry?" I ask him.

"That question means that *you're* hungry. What do you want? You can have anything."

"Pizza." I grin as my stomach growls. "With extra cheese, and I want breadsticks, too. With both ranch and marinara on the side."

"We can order that."

"And I want to eat it on the bed and watch reality TV. Like a dating show or something silly."

"You got it."

I blink at him. "That easy?"

"You're not exactly asking for the world here, sweetheart."

"I'M GOING to set you up on a date." Stella makes the announcement when I have my face stuffed with avocado toast and I can't reply to her, so I just raise an eyebrow. "Don't argue with me."

"Can't," is all I can say as I chew, and Stella grins at me.

"A bunch of us couples are going out for a game night, and I want you to join us."

"I'm not part of a couple," I remind her after swallowing.

"That's why I'm setting you up. It'll be a lot of fun, and you've met pretty much everyone going anyway."

"When is this happening?"

"Tonight."

I stop and stare at her, but Stella only grins.

"What, like you have big plans?"

"No." Honestly, I don't have plans at all because Keaton told me that he has to go hang out with his family tonight, so I was just going to stay home and write some more songs. "What if I hate the dude you've set me up with?"

"You won't, but if there's no spark, it's totally fine. He's a super laid-back guy. Mostly, it's so we can all hang out together and just have fun. No pressure."

When she puts it like that, it doesn't feel too scary.

"Okay, I'll go."

"*Yes.*" Stella pumps her fist in the air. "We'll leave around six."

"Where are we going? Should I get dressed up?"

"Definitely don't get dressed up. We're going to a place called Top Golf. Have you heard of it?"

"Yeah, it's like a bowling alley but for golf. I've never played golf in my life."

"Me, neither." Her smile doesn't falter. "It's gonna be a blast. And they have food and drinks there, too, so we can eat while we make total asses out of ourselves with the golf part."

"Great."

"IKE MIGHT BEAT us all at this," Stella says from the front seat of the car. Gray's driving us to the golf place, where we're apparently meeting the others.

Whomever the others are. They still haven't told me.

Except now I know that Ike and Sophie are one of the other couples.

"Ike's a football player. That doesn't mean he's good at golf," Gray points out.

"He's good at everything athletic," Stella counters with a bit of a pout. "He's even good at cornhole. He can do anything. But that's okay because we're just here to have fun."

Gray pulls into the parking lot and cuts the engine, and when we walk to the entrance, we find the others are already waiting for us.

Ike and Sophie are here, as expected. There's also Vaughn and Liv and the twin cousins, Josie and Maddie, who each have their guys with them, Brax and Dylan.

And the last person, standing just behind Liv, is Keaton Williams.

"Is Keaton my date?" I ask loud enough for everyone to hear.

"Yes," Liv confirms, clapping her hands. "We saw how well you two got along the other night when you arrived, and we thought it would be fun to set you up."

"Well, I know him," I reply and can't help but laugh. "You can't set me up with someone I *know*."

"Yes, we can," Liv insists, still smiling. "A blind date is a blind date."

I raise an eyebrow at Keaton. "Are you okay with being my partner tonight?"

"I guess I'll survive it." His lips tip up in that half smile I can't get enough of. "Come on, let's go kick their asses, Sid."

"You're not kicking my ass," Stella insists, shaking her head. "Not that we're here to be competitive."

"Competition is the Montgomery religion," Josie reminds us as Brax wraps his arm around her shoulder.

I like Brax a lot. He's a musician here in Seattle and has recently seen some success with his band. It's been fun to watch.

"I do believe that the Sterlings subscribe to the same religion," I say and nudge my brother with my elbow. "We can't let them beat us."

"There's more of them," Gray reminds me, but he smiles in that evil way he's done since he was a kid. "But we've got this."

"Nothing wrong with a little healthy competition," Ike says happily, holding Sophie's hand.

It's fun to see all of them coupled up, holding hands, and snuggling each other. They're obviously all in love, and there's no tension here at all. No one's fighting or jealous or pissy. They're all fun to hang out with.

I'm so glad I was invited to come tonight.

I glance over at Keaton, and a thought occurs to me. While Gray and Vaughn get us checked in, and the others are chatting away, I pull Keaton aside.

"So, you knew you were being set up on a date tonight?"

He shifts on his feet and sighs. "Yeah, I did."

"And you decided to come out on a blind date, even though you've been seeing *me.*"

His eyes narrow on me. "Looks like you did the same thing."

I laugh now and bump his hip with mine. "I'm just yanking your chain. I'm not mad. Wait, are *you* mad?"

"No." He shakes his head and leans down to whisper

in my ear. "I'm not mad. But this little outfit of yours turns me the hell on."

"How handy." I wink up at him, and then we're ushered to our bays, side by side. The attendant, clearly starstruck by Vaughn, helps us get our names set up in the computers, just like at a bowling alley.

"Wait, are you Sidney Sterling?" she asks, her eyes going even wider than they were before.

"Guilty," I reply with a smile as I quickly glance at her name tag. "Nice to meet you, Lacey."

"Holy shit, this is the best night at work *ever*. I'm not supposed to ask, but can I get a photo?"

"Why don't we do a group photo?" Stella asks. "Because you've got Brax Adler and Ike Harrison here, too."

"What?" Lacey just stares around at all of us, shocked. "How is this even possible? Yes, let's do a group photo! Let me get a coworker."

We spend the next fifteen minutes taking photos with Lacey, a group one and then a couple of individuals before she leaves us to play the game.

"She's sweet," Liv says with a smile but then glances at her brother. "You okay, Keat?"

For the first time, I notice that Keaton's face is hard, his hands fisted. He doesn't look happy *at all*.

"I'm fine. I just hate that shit."

"I know," Maddie says and pats his back. "But you did great. Besides, it was just one girl, and we made her whole month."

"I need a beer." Keaton glances at me. "You want a drink?"

"I'd love a margarita."

He nods sharply, and then he's gone, Gray on his heels.

"What was that about?" I ask Stella.

"Oh, Keaton *hates* the celebrity thing. He works really hard to stay out of any kind of spotlight and has since he was young. He's a lot like his dad in that way."

"What? Luke Williams is a big-time actor, producer, and director—you name it. He's as entrenched in Hollywood as it gets."

"But he doesn't live that lifestyle," Vaughn interrupts. "He hasn't acted in decades. He loves film, but he hates that world. He's kept his family in Seattle, not LA. And I get it."

"Keaton's just like Dad," Liv adds. "But even more so."

"Interesting," I mutter as the two men return, a waitress following them with a big tray loaded with drinks.

Once we all have a beverage and have ordered our food, we start playing the game. I just happen to be up first, so I grab the club and walk up to the little space with the ball.

I glance back at Keaton and wiggle my butt just a little before taking a swing at the ball.

I don't do well, but Stella was right. It *is* fun.

"Was that little wiggle for my benefit?" Keaton asks.

"All the other men are taken, so yeah, it was for you."

Liv snorts at that. "I'm so glad you two get along. I *knew* you would."

"Oh, we get along famously." I take a big sip of my drink and smile smugly over at Keaton. "He's rather fond of me."

"I hardly know you," he replies, and I don't know why, but that gets my back up.

"Is that so? You've seen me naked I don't know how many times, but you *hardly know me*?"

The room goes dead quiet, and I can feel everyone staring at us in surprise. Keaton's eyes stay steady on my own.

"You're kidding," Stella says at last.

"Finally," Sophie says, letting out a gusty breath. "I don't have to keep that secret anymore."

"We need *all* the dirt," Maddie puts in.

"I can't believe you just said that," Keaton mutters.

"Why? We're all adults here." I glance around the room and notice that my brother doesn't look very amused. "I'm not anyone's secret."

"I didn't say it was a secret."

I just smile at him, sip my drink, and glance over at Maddie's boyfriend, Dylan. "It's your turn, handsome."

"I think I'd rather watch this show than hit the ball," he says with a grin. "It's way more entertaining."

"Oh, there's nothing more to see. Keaton and I have a...thing going. That's all. It's not a secret. It's not illicit. It's consensual fun. Mostly *naked*, consensual fun."

"Jesus," Keaton mutters, making me laugh.

"He's shy." I wink at the others and pat Keaton's shoulder. "It's okay."

"I *knew* they had chemistry," Liv says again, doing the happy dance in her seat. "I just knew it."

"We're really good at matchmaking," Stella agrees and high-fives Liv.

I don't bother to remind them that Keaton and I found each other ourselves. They're having too much fun.

Finally, everyone goes back to eating and playing the game.

"I can't believe you did that," Keaton mutters next to me.

"I'm not going to sneak around to be with you," I reply, keeping my voice soft. "We're not doing anything wrong, Keaton."

"I didn't say we were."

"Great. We agree, then." I sip my drink happily.

Suddenly, my brother sits next to Keaton.

Before I can say anything, Keaton just shakes his head.

"Don't take a swing at me, man. I'm not a jerk who's playing around with your sister."

"I should punch you out of principle." Gray sighs and glances over at me. "But she's an adult. If you make her cry, I'll make you bleed."

"Right." Keaton takes a pull of his beer. "I figured that much."

"THAT WAS TOO FUN." I lean my head back against the seat in Keaton's Bronco and sigh. "I don't remember the last time I had that much fun."

"Are you sure you've never golfed before?"

I turn my head to smile at him. "I'm *very* sure. The margaritas were stronger than I expected. I have the nicest little buzz going."

"I'm glad."

"I want to see your house. Let's go there rather than my place."

He's suddenly quiet in the dark car as the street-lights zoom past, and I narrow my eyes at him.

"What's wrong?"

"I don't usually take girls to my house. It's nothing personal. I just don't."

"Yeah, well, you're with a woman now, and this woman wants to see where you live." My voice is firm, leaving no room for argument, and after a few moments, he nods.

"Okay, my house it is."

Satisfied, I settle back once more and enjoy the quiet as we drive through the city. Before long, we're headed *out* of the city.

"I assumed you lived in Seattle."

"On the outskirts," he confirms. "Not too far from my parents, if you take some back roads."

I watch as streetlights become fewer and farther between, and then Keaton turns off the main road onto a dirt driveway.

The house he pulls up to is *big*. With a sprawling, covered porch and even a tire swing in the front yard, it looks like there should be a big family living here.

"This seems big for one person."

"It is big," he confirms. "I bought it for the shop out back. Come on, I'll show you around."

It's dark, but he starts the tour outside. With my hand in his, he leads me around the house to what I assume must be the shop. It's two stories high, with four big garage doors, and when he leads me in through a small side door and turns on the lights, I let out a low whistle.

"This is really sexy, Keaton."

His eyes narrow as he takes it all in, as if he's seeing it for the first time with me. "Yeah, it is."

I can see why the building is so tall. It's to accommodate the lifts for the vehicles. There are two in here currently, and he has all kinds of tools, toolboxes, things with hoses and wires, and plenty of things I don't know anything about.

But I wasn't lying when I said that it's sexy as hell, and I plan to have sex in this building one day.

"Now, I want to see the house."

"It's far less sexy." He leads me out, turning off the

lights and locking the doors behind us. The walkway is concrete, and when we reach the back door, he opens it without unlocking it.

"You don't lock your doors?"

"Nothing in here to steal. You just saw the good stuff out there."

And when I walk through the mudroom and into the *enormous* kitchen, I can see that he's right. I've only seen a fraction of the house, and I can already tell that this is just where Keaton sleeps and showers. It's not a home at all.

"Such a bachelor pad," I mutter, shaking my head. "This kitchen is to die for, and there's nothing in it except old bananas and paper towels."

"I always buy too many bananas."

"Is the rest of the house this empty?"

"Pretty much."

I can't help but laugh as I follow him through a sparsely furnished living room. There's just a couch, a coffee table, and a TV. That's it.

"I'm shocked that your mom hasn't been in here, hanging stuff on the walls and such."

"She and my sisters threatened to, but I refused. It's fine like this for now."

I don't say anything as I follow him through the rest of the large house. All the guest rooms are completely empty. The owner's suite is big but only boasts a king-size bed and a nightstand.

I wander through the en suite bath and closet, both

also mostly empty, aside from a few clothes and a few personal things.

Finally, I turn and find Keaton leaning on the door-jamb of the bedroom, waiting for my reaction.

"I just have one question."

# CHAPTER 6

## KEATON

*S*he looks sexy as hell, standing in the middle of my bedroom in those tight jeans and red top that shows off her tits like the answer to a prayer. I haven't been able to take my eyes off her all night.

I'm not even mad that she told my family we're... doing whatever it is that we're doing.

In fact, after the initial surprise, it was actually damn funny. Sophie's relief made me laugh. My cousin has never loved keeping secrets, but that doesn't mean she's not good at it. She's like Fort Knox when it comes to being a confidant.

"What's your question, sweetheart?"

My feet remain planted here in the doorway. She's watching me with those sexy blue eyes, her lower lip caught between her teeth, and I want to cross to her, strip her bare, and pin her to the mattress. But first, I want to hear what's going on in that gorgeous head of hers.

"Does the furnace in this place work? Because I'm *freezing.*"

God, she makes me laugh.

I cross to her now, wrap my arms around her shoulders, and tug her against me for a long kiss. She fits against me so perfectly, as if her body was sculpted just for mine.

"I'll warm you up, babe."

"That's what I was hoping you'd say."

"WE REALLY NEED to put food in your fridge," Sidney says with a sigh as she turns on her side, naked and still a little sweaty, and cradles her head on her arm, watching me.

"Why?"

"Because I'm usually hungry after having adventurous sex, and I am not at all interested in eating those rotten bananas."

"I suspect that we'll be hanging out at your place most of the time."

"Why?" Her brows draw together in a frown, and I instinctively reach over and smooth those lines with my thumb.

"Because you have all the good food, silly."

That makes her chuckle. "If you really don't like having me come here, that's fine. My rental works."

"I don't mind having you here." I'm surprised to realize that it's true. I don't. I can't remember a time that I've ever brought a woman to my house. I always go back to their place or to a hotel. It's just cleaner that way.

But having Sidney in my bed isn't a hardship at all.

"I'll stock the pantry with some snacks. What's your favorite?"

"Wow, you'd do that for me? Hmm." She narrows her eyes, clearly giving the thought of post-coital snacks all her attention. "I want chips. Jalapeño chips. And cookies. Maybe throw in some frozen pizza, just in case."

"It's like shopping for a ten-year-old's birthday party."

"Yes, exactly! Have that in mind while you're shopping."

I can't help but chuckle before leaning over and gently kissing her lips.

"I have a question." She tugs the covers up over her shoulder and burrows down more snuggly in the bed.

"Ask away."

"Your sister and cousins told me earlier tonight that you don't like anything to do with fame."

"I want *nothing* to do with it," I confirm. "It makes me uncomfortable. Sometimes, it pisses me off."

"Fascinating." She plants her elbow under her head and rests her cheek on her palm. "Tell me more, please."

"It's why I was a little uncomfortable when you told the others that we're—"

"Friends with benefits?" The grin on her lips is smug.

"Yeah, that. I don't date celebrities, Sid. *Ever.* Been there, done that, burned the fucking T-shirt."

"That explains a lot," she admits. "But it doesn't change the fact that I won't be a secret."

"I wasn't trying to keep you a secret. I guess I don't want my family to think that I'm a hypocrite or that I've changed my mind when it comes to that. Because I *haven't* changed my mind. And as much as I enjoy being with you, whether we're naked or not, well…"

"This is as far as it can go for you. Because I'm a little famous."

"A little?" I smirk and can't resist reaching over to tug on a blonde strand. "You must not notice the glances you get in public when people recognize you."

"But *you* notice."

"Oh, yeah. It's not new to me. I'm Luke Williams's son, after all. My family is chocked full of people in the public eye, so whenever I'm out with them, we get looks."

"And that annoys you."

"Down to the marrow of my bones." I blow out a breath. "It's annoying when women flirt or act interested in me only because of who my father is. They don't want to date Keaton; they want Luke's son."

"Yeah, I can see how that would piss a person off," she agrees with a nod. "What about men? Is it hard to make friends?"

"I have a small circle. I'm lucky that I like my cousins so much because only they really understand what this life is like. And I have a couple of friends that I've had since grade school who I trust implicitly. And that's all I need. I'm sorry. I don't mean to hurt your feelings."

Her eyebrows climb, and she quickly shakes her head and sits up in the bed, holding the covers up to her chest.

"Are you kidding? It doesn't hurt my feelings. You're allowed to feel how you feel about anything at all. I don't really think of myself as a celebrity because there are so many iconic superstars in country music that are *super* famous, you know? Like Garth or Reba or Dolly… They are all household names. I just have to say their names, and you know exactly who I'm talking about."

"But you are definitely famous," I remind her.

"I've had success," she says slowly, that mind of hers whirling again. "But in the grand scheme of the business, I'm very mid-level, I guess you could say. Because, although I've done duets with some of the greats, and I've toured with them, I'm definitely not a household name. I can go to the grocery store or to the movies or just about anywhere without being recognized, especially if I don't wear makeup."

"You were recognized tonight."

"Yeah, but that's because we were with a whole group of famous people, Keaton. If it had just been you and me, I don't think that girl would have given me a second glance. She was aware because of Vaughn."

I purse my lips, thinking it over. "Maybe."

"Listen, I'm not trying to change your mind. I'm just speaking the truth here. I'm not even trying to change what's happening between the two of us. We're having a good time while I'm here. I know the rules."

She doesn't look mad or upset at all. She's just having an unusual conversation, and I can't help but find that *really* attractive.

Because some women would be trying to change the rules.

But not Sid.

"You're a beautiful, special woman, and I'm a lucky son of a bitch to be here with you."

"You're right, on all accounts." She lies down again and grins at me. "Stella invited me to the party at Leo and Sam's place over the weekend. Are you okay with that?"

"I was going to invite you myself."

That makes her eyes widen in surprise. "Really?"

"Sure. You should come. It's always a lot of fun."

"I *totally* want to come. Don't take this wrong, but Leo's kind of a big deal to me."

"Why would I take that wrong?"

"Because he's a *mega*-celebrity, and I'm having a tiny fangirl moment here. But I promise, I won't be a moron at his house. I'll keep it together."

"You're funny." I lean in to kiss her forehead. "You're no moron. I suspect just about any musician would geek out about spending time at his place."

"You *do* get it." She sighs in relief. "After our conversation, I didn't want you to roll your eyes and kick me out of your house."

"I rarely roll my eyes." I kiss her once more and then pull her against me. She rests her head on my chest, and it feels like everything shifts into place. "Get some sleep, baby."

She doesn't argue at all, just loops her arm around my stomach, and soon, I feel the long, even breaths coming from her in slumber.

"Dude, this is *Leo Nash's house!*" She's bouncing on the seat beside me as I pull into a parking space in front of the big stone house up on the cliffs, just north of Seattle. "I swear, I'm going to calm down and be sophisticated, but holy shit."

"You've sung with Reba, Rascal Flatts, and Blake Shelton. Hell, you even did a collab with Taylor Swift."

She whips her head around to stare at me. Her

pupils are dilated in excitement. "You pay attention, don't you?"

"Yeah, I do."

"Well, that all may be the case, and trust me when I say they're all *fantastic*, but this is Leo Nash, and even though I met him at your sister's wedding last year, I don't remember a word he said to me because my own voice kept screaming in my head, *THIS IS LEO NASH!*"

"You're cute." I lean over and kiss her cheek, then get out of the Bronco and walk around to open her door, where she's simply staring at the house, slack-jawed. "Are you coming inside, or are you planning to sit out here and stare at the house?"

"I'm coming." She takes my hand and hops out of the car. "Maybe I should have dressed up a little."

I take in her denim shorts and the yellow top that shows off her belly and ties between her breasts. She looks young, fresh, and classy-casual.

"There's nothing at all wrong with your outfit, babe."

I don't bother to knock as I push the door open, and we walk inside. The crowd will be out back, where there's an outdoor kitchen and dining area set up, along with tables and chairs, lawn games, you name it.

All while we take in the incredible view of Puget Sound.

"I hear them," I tell Sidney and smile down at her. She has a death grip on my hand. "I never pegged you as being shy."

"I'm not shy," she hisses. "I'm scared."

I stop short before anyone in the family sees us and pull her into a small bathroom before closing the door.

"Hold up." Sid's back is pressed to the closed door, and I cage her in with my arms. "Why in the hell are you scared? You're one of the most confident, outgoing women I know."

"A few reasons," she admits and takes a long, deep breath. "First, this is Leo's house. Second, I outed our relationship to your family a few days ago, and now I'm sure they all know."

"You said you wanted it that way."

"Of course, I want it that way." She frowns up at me. "But now they *know*."

"You're as confusing as you are beautiful."

"I don't want you to feel awkward with your family."

"Impossible. Now that we have that cleared up, what else are you afraid of?"

She takes a minute, licks her lips, and then says, "I think that's it."

"Then you have nothing to worry about." I kiss her lightly at first, and then I sink in while framing her face in my hands. When I pull back, all the worry is gone from her face, and her blue eyes shine with lust. "That's as far as we're going in here."

"Then you shouldn't have gotten me all worked up." She pushes at my chest, and I back up with a grin. "Come on, let's go rip off the bandage."

"You've met everyone here," I remind her. "And if you feel uncomfortable at all, which I can't imagine because this is my family we're talking about, and they adopt everyone, come find me and hold my hand. I'm not going anywhere."

Her shoulders drop in relief. "Thanks. Really. Okay, I'm ready."

I poke my head out of the bathroom to make sure no one's lurking about to witness us coming out of here. But there's no one around, and I can still hear the others in the back.

"Let's go." I take her hand in mine and lead her through the house, into the kitchen, where several of the moms are filling platters and talking up a storm.

"Hey, Mom, aunts." Mom's eyes brighten with interest when she sees that I'm holding Sidney's hand. "I hope you made lots of food because I'm starving."

"Your uncle Will and Ike are here," my aunt Meg says as she wipes her hands on a towel and crosses over to hug me. "They can eat a third-world country out of house and home. Trust me, we have plenty."

"Stella and Gray are out back," Aunt Jules says with a wink. "Along with everyone else."

"We put up a volleyball net," Aunt Sam puts in. "I think there's going to be a tournament."

"I'd better go check it out."

"How are you, Sidney?" Mom asks.

"Oh, I'm doing very well. Thanks for asking. And

thanks for inviting me today. There's never a dull moment at a Montgomery party."

"You catch on fast," my aunt Brynna says with a laugh. "Have fun, you two."

"Oh, they're gorgeous together," I hear Aunt Jules say as we walk out the door, and I choose not to acknowledge the comment.

Sidney tightens her grip on my hand and lets out a little giggle.

"You're enjoying this."

"Oh, for sure. But let's be honest, we *are* gorgeous together." She winks up at me and then waves at her brother as he and Stella see us. "Hi, guys!"

"Get some food, and come join us," Stella invites.

"She doesn't have to tell me twice," I mutter as I lead Sid over to the buffet under a tent. "The family is so big now, Sam and Leo have to put up this tent for the food. They didn't use to when I was a kid."

"Do they rent it?"

"Hell no. They bought the tent and all the tables and chairs, and Leo had a shed built to store it all in. There's always a crew of us family that comes before the party to help set up. Those who don't set up stay to tear down."

"Looks like we'll be staying to tear down," she says as she slaps some potato salad onto her plate.

"Oh, you don't have to—"

"We will stay and help." Her voice leaves no room for argument.

"Yes, ma'am."

With full plates, we walk over to join Stella and Gray.

"Why are you two all alone?" Sid asks.

"Everyone else is playing volleyball," Gray says. "We decided to play the winners."

"You think you're that good, huh?" I ask him as I sit and dig into a rib.

"Gray played in college," Sidney says with pride in her voice. "He was kind of a big deal."

"Did you play beach volleyball in those little Speedos?" Stella wants to know.

"No."

"Too bad." Stella shrugs a shoulder and turns her attention back to her food. "Did you guys just get here?"

"Yeah," Sidney says. "I was nervous, so I dragged my feet getting ready."

"Why are you nervous?" Stella asks, but Gray just smiles at his sister.

"Because we're at Leo's house," he answers for her. "And Leo is probably her all-time biggest hero."

"Aside from Dolly, yes," Sidney confirms. "I don't want to make an ass out of myself."

"Oh, you won't." Stella waves that off. "Trust me, everyone here is normal. You know that. You've already met everyone, including Leo."

"I know, it's just…different. I don't usually get

starstruck. Hardly *ever*, in fact. But this one makes me a little weird."

"We all have that *one*," Stella says with a nod.

"Who's yours?" Gray wants to know. "I figured you'd be immune to celebrities."

"Let's clarify something first," Stella says. "Are we talking about celebs we can have a hall pass for or just celebs that we love and might have a meltdown if we ever met them?"

"Wait, are you saying that my *uncle* Leo is your fucking hall pass?" I scowl down at Sidney, who just grins up at me.

"I'm pleading the fifth."

"That's just disturbing," I mutter.

"Either one," Gray says, responding to Stella's question.

"Okay, my hall pass is Paul Rudd." She waggles her eyebrows.

"He could be your father," Sidney says in horror.

"But he's not," Stella reminds her. "Besides, I'm pretty sure my uncle Leo could be *yours*."

"Stop grossing me out while I'm eating," I complain, making them all laugh.

"Okay, who's *your* hall pass?" Sidney asks me.

"I don't have one."

"That's right, Keaton doesn't like celebrities," Stella says with a grin and turns to her fiancé. "What about you?"

"I have the woman of my dreams," he replies easily. "I don't need a hall pass."

"Okay, that was a good answer," Sidney says with a grin. "Look at my brother, being all smooth and charming."

"It's a talent," Gray replies with a laugh.

"Hi, you guys." Aunt Samantha approaches our table, a big smile on her face. My aunt Sam is one of my favorite people in the world. She and Leo didn't have kids. So, instead, they mentor and treat all of us cousins as if we're theirs.

It doesn't suck.

"How was the food?" she asks.

"Damn good," I reply. "What's for dessert?"

"Your aunt Nic brought a million cupcakes." She winks at me and then sets her hand on Sidney's shoulder. "Hey, Leo and Brax and a few others are up in the studio, jamming. They just called down and asked me to send you up there, Sid."

Sidney's jaw drops. "Oh, I don't think—"

"Don't be stupid," I whisper in her ear. "That's awesome. You should go up."

She swallows hard and looks back up at Sam. "Are you sure they want *me* up there? I don't want to interrupt."

"Honey, I don't know if you've heard, but you're kind of a big deal in Nashville." Sam's eyes sparkle as she steps back so Sidney can stand up from the table. "They absolutely want you to join them."

Sid looks down at me. "You're coming with me. I'm too nervous to go up there alone."

"Keaton knows the way," Sam says with a wink. "Have fun. Then come down and play for the rest of us."

Sidney looks shell-shocked as Sam walks away.

"Is this really happening?"

"No sleeping with Uncle Leo," Stella throws out there. "Hall passes aren't real."

That makes Sidney laugh. "Thanks. I needed that laugh. Okay, here we go. Wait, I'll follow you. I don't know where I'm going."

"I'll lead the way."

I take her hand and lead her back into the house and past the kitchen, where several family members have congregated. No matter whose house we're partying at, the kitchen always seems to be the center of the action.

Sid tightens her hand in mine as I lead her up the stairs to Leo's studio.

"This isn't happening," I hear her mutter, but I don't answer.

The red recording light is off above the door, so I open it, and we step inside. This is a full-functioning recording studio, with instruments and a sound booth. Several Nash albums have been recorded here, along with other famous performers' albums when they've come to collaborate with Leo.

Sidney's smile is a mile wide as she takes it all in.

"There you are," Leo says, waving us in. "Brax and I have been playing with some music, but we need a female's perspective. And I'm glad you came up, Keaton, because we need someone on the keys."

Sidney spins around and gapes up at me. "You can *play*?"

"A little."

"A lot," Leo says, rolling his eyes. "Come on, we have work to do."

# CHAPTER 7

## SIDNEY

*K*eaton can *play*.

Not just a little bit, either. This man plays better than some of the people I've toured with, and that's saying a lot.

I could sit and watch him play all day.

"Do you need a guitar?" Leo asks me, after watching me play an imaginary one while I sing. I can't help it. I'm used to playing while I brainstorm, whether it's a guitar or a piano.

I beat the habit while I'm on stage.

"Sure, if you have a spare. I just think better with it, if that makes sense."

"Makes complete sense," Brax says with a grin. "Hey, I want to just say that I'm a fan of your work, Sidney. I didn't say anything before because there wasn't a good time, and I didn't want to embarrass you or put you on the spot in front of the others, but I really love your music."

"Thank you." I feel my cheeks flush the way they always do when someone compliments my music. "And likewise. I'm loving your new album."

"Okay, as much as I can appreciate this conversation, the mutual lovefest is over," Leo says with a grin. "Let's *play.* I've been on hiatus for a while, and I need some time with other musicians. Sam's probably going to make us go downstairs at some point to play for everyone."

I grin over at Keaton, who's been waiting patiently behind the baby grand piano. There's also a complex keyboard system in here, but Keaton said he prefers the piano.

"Okay, I like the second verse, but what if you did this instead?" I rest the guitar Leo offered me on my thigh and, from memory, begin to play the melody that Leo and Brax have already played at least a dozen times, but I switch up the lyrics a bit.

"Oh, that's good," Leo says, nodding and picking up the chorus with me.

Brax and Keaton join in, and for the next hour, we write an absolutely gorgeous song that has my creative juices flowing and energy bouncing off me.

"This is my favorite part of my job," I admit with a grin when we take a break from the song. "The creation of it all."

"Do you sing many of your own songs?" Leo asks.

"Almost all the songs on my albums have been mine," I reply with a nod. "Sometimes they're a collaboration, and usually one or two of the tracks are written by someone else. But I've always been lucky that the producers have liked my songs."

"Are you taking requests?" Brax asks with a grin.

"Sure. What do you want to hear?"

"'Life in the Slow Lane'. It's my favorite of yours."

I grin and strum the strings, pulling the song to the forefront of my brain. This one is from my second album and has always been a fan favorite.

"Sure." I clear my throat and begin to play it on the guitar. After a few beats, Keaton joins me on the piano, which surprises me. He's watching me with those calm, intense green eyes.

It's damn intimate.

Leo and Brax both sit back and listen as I sing my way through the ballad that I wrote when I was home between tours what feels like so many years ago. I'd been *so* homesick, and I wanted to stay there, in my childhood home on the lake, forever.

When the song's over, and the last notes disappear into the air, the three men erupt into applause, making me laugh.

"If we're going to play more of our backlists, we'd better go downstairs and do it for everyone," Leo says with a sigh. "I have the sound equipment set up."

"Do you always perform live shows at family gatherings?" I ask as Leo and Brax grab their guitars.

"When we host, yes," Leo says. "Sometimes my band comes with their families, too."

"Wow. That sounds like fun."

He grins at me. "It is. You'll have to come to the next one."

I blink and glance over at Keaton, who's listening and smiling at me with that sexy half smile.

"Thanks. If I'm in town, I'd love it."

"Hey, listen," Leo says as Brax and Keaton start talking about cars. "I don't want to overstep here, or say something unwelcome, but if you ever need anything, don't hesitate to reach out to me. I've been a fan of yours for a while, too, and I'm always here if you want to cowrite or if you need anything at all."

And just like that, I have to blink quickly so the tears that threaten don't spill over.

"Thank you so much. That means a lot to me, coming from you, Leo. You've been a musical hero of mine for a long time. I'm just happy to be here, honestly."

"I'm happy to have you. And you know what? That song we wrote today? You should take it. Tweak it and make it your own. You did most of the work on the lyrics anyway."

"Oh, I couldn't do that."

"You should," Brax insists. "It's definitely a Sidney Sterling song. It suits you."

"And it won't make you mad if I put my own spin on it?"

"Not at all. That's what we do." Leo winks at me. "Take that guitar down with you. If you think you're getting out of performing for the family, you've lost your mind."

"Is Starla here today?" Brax asks.

"Nah, she and Levi are in LA. She's recording down there."

"Wait." I hold my hands up. "*Starla*? Like, *the* Starla?"

"Sure," Keaton says. "She's married to one of our cousins, and they're usually here, too."

"Just when I think this family can't get any more interesting," I mutter as Keaton winks and gestures for me to lead the way out of the studio. Leo's the last to leave and locks up behind us.

I follow the others to an area outside that I didn't notice before. It's a little patio off to the side with rock benches, where a small sound system is set up, complete with mics and pedal boards for the guitars.

There's even a keyboard set up, along with a set of drums.

"Do we have a drummer?" I ask.

"Hudson," Brax says with a grin and then searches the yard for the younger man. "He was coming late because he had to work. There he is. I'll go get him."

"Hud has a summer job, working for his dad's construction company," Keaton informs me. "My uncle Mark has hired him every summer since he was fifteen. He's a hell of a drummer."

"He's been drinking too much," Leo says, narrowing his eyes.

"Didn't we all at that age?" Keaton asks with a laugh. "He'll grow out of that shit."

"Hey, guys, sorry I missed the jam sesh," Hudson, who looks like a younger version of all the Williams brothers, with a sculpted jaw, muscles for days, and a devastatingly charming smile, hurries over our way. He's also tall and already nice and tanned from working outside so much. "Oh, hi, Sidney. It's good to see you again."

Add polite to the long list of things he has going for him.

"You, too. I hear you're pretty good with the sticks."

"Hell yeah. Uncle Leo will let me go on tour with him sooner or later."

"Dude, I have a drummer. He'd be pretty pissed if I tried to replace him." Leo ruffles Hudson's hair and passes him a set of sticks.

"What are we playing?" Hudson asks. "Anything specific, or are we taking requests again?"

"Requests are fun," Keaton says but then frowns. "Hey, Hud, do you know any of Sid's songs?"

"Are you kidding? After I met her at Liv's wedding last year, I learned a bunch of her stuff. Now that she's in the family, I have to know, for days like this."

I'm so taken by surprise that all I can do is just stare at the younger man. "I'm not—"

"Sure, you are," Hudson interrupts with a big smile. "Your brother is marrying Stella. You're family now."

"Oh." I glance at Keaton, who's smiling at me again.

"That's how we do things around here," he says, as if it's no big deal at all.

"Been that way since the beginning of time," Leo confirms. "This crew brought Meg and me into the family so fast, our heads spun."

"You and Meg are related? That's Will's wife, right?"

"Yeah, it's a long story," Leo says. "But, without boring you with all the details, she's pretty much my sister. The Montgomery and Williams clan brings everyone into the fold, whether you're here by blood, marriage, or even friendship. There's always room for more."

"Damn. That's really sweet. I wish Maya was here. My sister would love this."

"Next time," Leo says again with a wink and then walks up to the mic. "Okay, everyone, we're gonna play for a while. We're taking requests, so if there's something specific you want to hear, just call it out."

"'Life in the Slow Lane,'" someone yells, and Leo grins over at me.

"You ready?"

I take a deep breath, looking out at the dozens of people watching us, all of them here because they belong to this amazing family, and nod.

"Ready."

I've sung for politicians, movie stars, and royalty.

But I've never been as nervous as I am right now.

But then I see my brother smiling at me, Stella snuggled up to his side, and everything in me calms.

These are my people.

Leo plays the intro on his guitar, Keaton and Hudson join in, and the next thing I know, I'm singing my song with these men backing me up, who clearly know the song very well.

How is this even possible?

After the first thirty minutes of playing a mix of mine, Leo's, Brax's, and even freaking *Starla's* music, Leo decides he's too hot and strips out of his black T-shirt, exposing those tattooed stars on his hips that have been front and center of many a fantasy of mine for *years*.

Holy shit.

My gaze catches Stella's, and she's laughing at me, as if she can read my mind.

And I can't help but laugh with her.

"Come on up here, Meg," Leo says into the mic. He grins when he sees Meg walking through the crowd to the small stage. "Hey there, Meg Pie."

"Hi." Meg grins and picks up a mic. "You guys sound great tonight."

"With this crew? We can't go wrong. What do you want to sing?" Leo asks her.

"Let's go with an oldie. How about 'Kiss Me Slowly'?"

"Let's do it."

I drift off to the side and just listen. They don't need my harmony as they sing the song flawlessly, their voices meshing so perfectly, it almost makes a person want to cry.

"Why don't you sing together all the time?" I ask when the song is over.

"We used to," Meg says with a grin. "But then I went to nursing school, and Leo went off and got famous without me."

"Let's not start that again," Leo says, shaking his head.

"He gets touchy," Meg says with a laugh. "Okay, you guys keep going. I'm only good for one song these days."

She waves and walks back over to her husband, the former football superstar Will Montgomery, and he just picks her right up and kisses the hell out of her.

This family fascinates me.

"Let's hear another one of Sidney's songs," someone calls out.

"Come on, you're not done yet," Leo says with a grin. "Are you having fun?"

"I don't know when I've ever had more fun in my life."

"Good."

"I DON'T REMEMBER the last time I was this revved up about music." Keaton's driving us back to my condo, his Bronco gliding smoothly on the freeway in the dark, and I can't stop moving in my seat. "I know that sounds crazy because music is my whole job, but, man, I feel like I could go home and write about a million songs tonight."

"It was fun," he agrees and reaches over to take my hand, lifting it to his lips. "You're damn talented, Sid."

"Me?" I giggle and pull *his* hand to *my* lips. "You shocked the hell out of me with your keyboard skills. How do you know all my songs? And all the other ones you played tonight?"

"I didn't know them," he admits with a shrug. "Not really. I mean, I know your music, but I've never played them before."

"What are you, some kind of savant?"

He doesn't answer as he takes the exit off the freeway toward my building.

"Seriously, Keaton."

"I have a knack," he says at last. "I wanted to learn martial arts when I was a kid, and my mom made me a deal. If she agreed to pay to let me get beat up, I also had to take lessons for an instrument. I chose the piano."

"How did martial arts go?"

"I'm a black belt in Judo."

I blink over at him as he parks the Bronco in my

space. I don't have a car, so he can use the one space I'm allowed. It works.

"So, you play the piano like a pro, *and* you're a black belt. Like I said, you're a savant."

He doesn't answer me as he exits the vehicle, then walks around and opens my door, holding out a hand to help me out. I learned early on with Keaton that he's a door opener.

I don't have a problem with that.

He leads me upstairs and to my door without saying anything.

And when I've keyed in the door code and opened it, I pull him inside with me, just in case he's lost his mind and thinks that he isn't going to spend the night with me.

"What else can you do?" I demand as I immediately walk into the kitchen and pour us each a glass of wine.

"What do you mean?" he asks, accepting the glass. He sits on the couch, and I curl up on the chair directly across from him so I can see his face while I ask questions.

"Come on... Piano. Judo. What else?"

He sips his wine thoughtfully. "I also play the guitar, and I thought about playing baseball in college, but then I decided that college wasn't for me, so I went to a vo-tech school to learn about cars."

"You play guitar."

He shrugs. "It's not a big deal, you know. I have an

artistic family, so I was never lacking in help if I needed it."

"I'm impressed," I admit and sip my wine. "You can play songs by ear, without any sheet music. *And* you're a badass, with the whole Judo thing."

"Yes, I'm a total badass."

He smirks and waves it off, but I just shake my head at him.

"And you're modest, too."

"What's your favorite car?" he asks, completely out of the blue.

"Huh?"

"You've learned a *lot* about me today, but there's still so much I don't know about you. What's your favorite car?"

"I don't know if I've ever thought about it. I don't have a car."

That makes him frown and lean forward in his seat. "What do you mean, you don't have a car?"

"I don't need one. I'm gone a lot, and when I'm on tour, I have a driver that's been with me for *years.* If I need to go somewhere in Nashville, like to run errands or something, he drives me."

"Do you have a license?"

"Of course." I grin at him.

"Okay, this is so far out of the realm of normal for me, my head is spinning." He sets his wine aside. "If you could buy any car, what would you buy?"

"I don't know. I think I would want an SUV or a

truck so that I'm sitting up high. I don't like cars that sit low to the ground."

"Now we're narrowing it down. Is there a brand that you like?"

I frown, thinking it over. "My friend Miranda has a Porsche Cayenne. That's a sweet car."

"A damn sweet car," he agrees. "Is that Miranda Lambert?"

I smile smugly. "She lives not too far from me. I guess I'd buy one of those, but I don't have any idea how much they cost."

"They're in the six figures."

I choke on my wine. "For a *car*?"

That makes him laugh. "Honey, that's not just a car. That's a fucking experience. If the rumble doesn't make you come when you're driving, you're doing it wrong."

"I can honestly say that riding in Miranda's car has never given me an orgasm."

"That vehicle is wasted on her."

"Stella told me once that you've restored cars for the likes of Jay Leno and Matthew McConaughey."

"Among others."

"How much did they pay for those cars?"

"I signed nondisclosure agreements," he replies. "I could tell you, but then I'd have to kill you."

"Come on." I cross to him and sit in his lap. "You know I won't tell anyone."

"Can't do it."

"Was it more than the Cayenne?"

"Quite a bit more, yes."

I raise an eyebrow. "Double?"

He clears his throat and plants his hands on the globes of my ass. "Give or take."

"Wow, that's a lot. What kind of car do you think I should drive?"

He inhales sharply, as if just the thought of it turns him on.

"1969 Corvette Stingray ZL-1."

"That's incredibly specific."

"It's a honey of a car and rare. Sexy. Smart. Handles like a fucking dream. It's you, in car form."

"Maybe I should buy one."

That makes his lips turn up in the corners. "If you have an extra three million hanging around, I say go for it."

My jaw drops. "Three *million*? Dollars?"

"Not pesos, I'll tell you that."

"Why is it so expensive?"

"It's very rare."

"Have you ever seen one?"

"Yes."

"Have you driven it?"

"Yes."

I tilt my head to the side in interest. "Whose did you drive?"

"I can't tell you."

"Ah, that pesky NDA thing again."

"Yes, ma'am."

I chew my lip, watching him. God, he's fucking incredible. Sexy as hell, smart, gifted. He makes me laugh and makes me feel safe.

He's the best thing that's come into my life in a very long time.

"What are you thinking?" He brushes my hair off my face and drags his fingertips down my cheek.

"I think we should get naked."

Sex distracts me from how much I enjoy him *outside* of the bedroom.

And all the reasons that it's a bad idea.

# CHAPTER 8

## KEATON

"*W*hat—and I mean this in the most loving way possible—in the actual fuck?"

I open one eye and peer up at my cousin, Liam, whose Hawaiian shirt could scorch the corneas of a blind man from a mile away.

"What?" I slip my sunglasses on and scowl up at him. Liam and I are the same age and were pretty much raised as siblings, just like all the cousins.

We also couldn't be more different.

Where I tend to be quiet and reserved, Liam is boisterous and outgoing. He's never met a stranger. And he's not afraid, not in the least, to speak his mind.

"Why is it that we're all here, every single male member of this family, at Uncle Will's casita, and you're lying on this chair, sleeping like a goddamn sloth?"

"The last time I checked, we come here to *relax*. Not that you know the meaning of the word."

Liam scoffs, kicks my chair, and flips me off when I yell, "Hey!"

"Get your lazy ass up and come join us for some ping-pong."

"No." I lie back, eyes closed again, and then suddenly, I'm in the air. Chair and all, I'm hefted into the air and headed toward the water. "Put me the fuck down. What is wrong with you assholes?"

But before I can jump off, I'm tossed into the pool, and when I come up sputtering and drenched, Liam, Drew, Ike, and Hudson are all laughing like a bunch of loons.

"You're all going to pay for that."

The threat only makes them laugh harder, but Ike has the decency to offer me a hand to help me out of the pool.

Instead, I plant my feet on the side and pull him in with me, much to the hilarity of my cousins, including those who have joined us.

"You're all a bunch of assholes."

"Come on," Drew says and, stifling his laughter, really helps me out of the pool. "You have to wake up, or you'll miss all the good stuff."

I wasn't sleeping. I was listening to the conversations going on around me. I'm quiet because I like to take everything in and absorb what's being said. If I make eye contact, people want to pull me into conversations.

Which is fine, but sometimes, all the chaos gets overwhelming.

And with a family the size of mine, chaos is the norm. Will invited all the men in the family over for some fun, since the weather is so nice. The only guy missing today is Vaughn because he's in LA on location.

"What did I miss?" I accept a towel from my dad, who's also laughing, and wipe it over my face. It's nice enough today in the sunshine that I'll dry off quickly.

And if need be, I have a change of clothes in my Bronco.

"Uncle Will is about to give us some inside dirt on the team," Drew says. "But he only wants to tell the story once."

I glance at Ike, who's still standing nearby. "Do you know the dirt?"

"Dude, of *course,* I know." Ike shakes his head and walks ahead of me to the covered patio, which isn't a normal-sized patio, but rather a giant outdoor space that Will had built about ten years ago so we could have parties like this one.

I hover just outside, where the sun can still hit me and dry me off.

"Is everyone here?" Will asks, glancing around.

"We woke up Keaton," Liam says with a smug grin. "Now, spill the beans, Uncle Will."

"The team finally sold," Will begins, and all of us go still.

"Did the family buy it?" Hudson asks.

No one in our family is a billionaire on their own. But combined? Yeah, it would be possible for the family to invest together and own a professional football team.

"No," Uncle Luke says. "We thought about it, and had plenty of family meetings about it, but we decided to pass."

"Damn," Finn says, shaking his head. "Inheriting a piece of a pro team one day would have been cool."

"What the hell are you talking about?" Matt, Finn's dad, counters. "We're all going to live forever."

"Right." Finn smirks, and Will keeps talking.

"So, some billionaire bought the team?" Uncle Caleb asks. "Who is it?"

"It's a brother and sister team, Rome and London Ambrose."

"They're not billionaires," Uncle Dom says with a frown.

"No, but their father is." Will shrugs. "I'm sure he put up a big chunk of the money, but Rome and London are listed as the owners."

"Aren't they known for being computer geeks?" Uncle Nate asks. "What do they know about football?"

"Probably not much," Ike mutters next to me, as he's also standing in the sun to dry off.

"They're the money behind it," Will says calmly.

"They don't have to know the game to put up the money to buy the team. I'm the one who has that knowledge, and they've asked me to take on the role of general manager and president of operations for the organization."

We're all stunned silent for a moment, and then there are whoops and cheers of excitement.

"As it damn well should be," Uncle Isaac says and claps his brother on the back. "You know more about that team, and the game in general, than anyone else could."

"There's always something to learn," Will says. "And I haven't accepted the position yet."

"What?" My dad scowls at Will and crosses his arms over his chest. "Why the hell not?"

Will exhales and rubs his hands over his face. I don't believe that he invited all the men in the family over for one of his guys' day parties just to get our opinions on if he should take the job of a lifetime.

But maybe he needs to talk it through.

"I know that Meg wouldn't have put up a fight on this one," Leo says quietly, leaning on the tile counter of the outdoor kitchen. "She's always supported the hell out of you."

"And she supports this, too. Whatever I decide. I don't know… I spent so many years traveling with the team, being gone for long lengths of time. I hated being away from the girls and missing out on my nieces' and nephews' important moments, too. If I take this job, it'll be full time again. No more working as a consultant or commentating on the weekends here in Seattle."

"You didn't anticipate coming out of retirement," Nate guesses.

"No. I didn't. I like calling my own shots and being available to my family. Sure, the girls are grown and out on their own now, but I've been having a good time with my wife."

"She still works full time," Uncle Dom reminds him.

"Actually, she went part time about a year ago," Will says. "And we planned to start traveling for *fun*. So, I don't know... It's a lot to think about."

"I know I'm new here," Dylan says, catching everyone's attention. "And it's not exactly my place to give you advice, especially when you haven't even asked for any."

"You're family," Will says simply. "Everyone is welcome to speak. What's on your mind, Dylan?"

"You *love* football. It's not just a hobby or a former job; you live it. You've helped the team for years since you retired—for *free*. The players trust you."

Dylan looks over to Ike, who simply nods.

"Seems to me, with the new owners not knowing jack squat about the game, the team and the staff would be more comfortable with you in a leadership role. It doesn't mean you have to commit to it forever. You could even state that you only want a three, or hell, even a one-year contract to start."

"I was going to say the same thing," I add, nodding. I

shift on my feet when all eyes turn to me. "Dylan's right. It would help the transition for the team, give them some stability and confidence."

"It doesn't have to be another twenty years of your life," Uncle Mark adds quietly. "It doesn't have to be as difficult as you're making it."

Will chews on his lower lip, thinking it over. "I've never really been someone to overthink every little detail, but maybe that's what I've done here."

"If Rome and London—which, by the way, only rich people name their kids after cities—want to bring you on, I say do it. And ask for a fuck ton of money," Caleb says. "Because you'll earn it, and you're worth it."

"I wonder how much a *fuck ton* of money is," Gray ponders, speaking for the first time. Most of us kids have just been listening.

"Well into the eight figures," Nate says, his eyes narrowed.

Several of us whistle at that, and Will grins. "I guess I could use a little extra cash."

"Just some pocket change," Dad says with a smirk.

"I honestly didn't intend to ask for advice today," Will says. "But thanks for giving it. I'll double-check with Megan and make sure she's still on board, but I think I'll take the job."

"Thank fuck," Ike says, making everyone laugh.

"I wondered why you were so damn quiet," Will says, grinning at the younger quarterback and Will's protégé.

"Because I didn't trust myself not to beg," Ike replies. "Dylan's right. Everyone will feel a lot better about the situation if we have you there with us."

"No pressure or anything," Drew adds with a grin.

"I wanted to speak with you and planned to do it alone, but this is as good a time as any," Will says to Drew. "With more than five years of coaching experience, I want to hire you as the defensive line coach."

Drew's jaw drops, and his dad, Caleb, looks so fucking proud, I'm surprised his chest doesn't explode.

"I only have college coaching experience," Drew reminds his uncle.

"You have plenty of experience," Will says. "You have excellent instincts and a good comradery with players. They respect you."

"I'm only twenty-seven," Drew counters.

"Are you trying to talk him out of it?" Leo asks Drew.

"I just don't want to be offered the job because I'm Will Montgomery's nephew and share the same last name. Besides, I still have one more year on my contract at the University of Seattle."

"I bet we can buy that out," Will says with confidence.

"Would it be a lot more money, moving to the pros?" Hudson asks.

"Probably double the money. Seven figures," Will says, still watching Drew, who's starting to look hopeful. "And who gives a fuck what people say about us being related? If you were a pissy coach, I wouldn't hire you."

"Let me do some thinking," Drew says slowly as he shoves his hands into his pockets. "And thank you. Really, thanks for trusting me with that. I just have to think. You kind of sprung this on me."

"You'd be damn good at it," Caleb says to his son.

"You have to say that. You're my dad."

"I don't have to say shit," Caleb says, in that brusque way he has.

"Uncle Caleb says it like it is," Liam reminds us. "If you were an asshole, he'd call you an asshole."

That makes us all smirk.

"I think it's time to break out some beer and celebrate," Isaac announces.

"Or wine," Dom says with a wink. "We have both. For the record, I'm proud of you, Will."

"Don't get mushy," Finn says, cringing. "And bring on the beer."

"Not for you," Matt tells his son, clapping him on the shoulder. "You're still a minor."

"It was worth a try."

"WHY WOULD you hesitate to take that awesome job?" Liam asks Drew. We're sitting on the far side of the pool, eating the barbecue that Uncle Will had catered. Uncle Matt and Isaac round out the five of us.

There are Montgomery men all over this place.

And that's what we all are, no matter the last name.

"I have to think of my team," Drew says, picking at the potato salad with a fork on his plate. "I'm two years in on this contract, and I've just established a rapport with my guys. A routine."

"College players rotate in and out often," Isaac says.

"True, but we have a few guys who won't go pro but who are excellent college players and leaders for the others. I like my job a lot. But working for a pro team has always been my goal, and the fact that I'm being offered a job to lead a defensive line before I'm thirty? That's just wild."

"Not to mention more money," Liam says. "You have the chops for it."

"The press is going to *slaughter* me," Drew says with a sigh. "Because Will and I are related. He can blow that off all he wants, but it's going to be a pain in the ass."

"Our family has dealt with the press forever," Matt points out. "And I say let them talk. Who the fuck cares? You'll do the job well, and after a while, they won't have anything to bitch about."

"It'll blow over," I add.

"That's coming from the guy who avoids the press like the plague," Drew says with a laugh.

"I didn't say it would be fun."

"I'll probably take it if Will accepts the job he's offered and presents me with an official offer. I would be stupid as hell to pass on it."

"You'll do what's right for you," Matt says simply, then turns to me. "And speaking of staying out of the spotlight, you're sure flirting with it a lot lately."

"How so?"

"We all have eyes," Isaac replies. "We saw you with Gray's sister at Leo's party last week. You always swore you'd stay away from anyone famous, and here you are, giving the gooey eyes to a music star."

"I was *not* giving her gooey eyes."

"Oh, you totally were," Liam confirms with a grin. "It was *so sweet*."

He makes kissy noises, and I throw an empty rib bone at him, making him laugh.

I don't know if Liam will ever grow up.

"She's beautiful," Matt continues, ignoring Liam. "Legs for days."

"I think her legs are her brand," Drew adds. "She's always wearing those short denim shorts in her videos and stuff. Short skirts on stage. I think that's her thing."

She *does* have killer legs. And when they're wrapped around my waist, there's nothing better in the fucking world.

But I don't tell them that.

"She's my friend," I say simply and reach for the beer I grabbed with my food and take a sip.

"With benefits?" Isaac asks with a knowing grin.

I just look steadily at the older man but don't answer.

"That's a yes," Liam says, but he doesn't whoop and

holler or make it a big deal. "Good for you, man. I like her, all jokes aside."

"She's not my girlfriend or anything," I reply quietly. "We're friends who have a good time together. That's it."

"Why?" Matt asks.

"Because you said it yourself. She's famous. End of story."

"For fuck's sake," Isaac mutters, shaking his head. "Youth is wasted on idiots like you."

"I love you, too."

Isaac smirks and reaches over to ruffle my hair, the way he's done since I was a toddler.

"You're a smart idiot," he clarifies. "Too smart sometimes."

"You're both consenting adults," Matt points out with a shrug of his shoulder. "If sex is all you want, that's fine. Nothing wrong with that."

Matt's always been very blunt and open when it comes to sex, especially with us boys. All our dads are, but I think of Matt as a college professor when it comes to sex. I suspect that he has some secrets that he doesn't share with the rest of the family.

But I learned a long time ago not to ask him questions he doesn't want to answer. He's a freaking vault.

"Do we have dessert?" Drew wonders, effectively changing the subject.

I grin over at him, and he just gives me a knowing nod.

"I heard someone say something about pie. No idea what kind," Isaac says as Drew jumps up, carrying his empty plate.

"I'll go scout it out," Drew promises. "I have to get over there before Uncle Will eats it all."

"I'll go with you," Liam says.

"I need more ribs," Isaac adds and follows the other two toward the buffet line, leaving me alone with Matt.

"Don't let your hang-ups about fame destroy a really great connection with a beautiful woman," he says, not even looking my way.

"I can't deal with that life." It's really as simple as that.

"You *can*," he says. "You don't want to. There's a big difference."

"Can't or won't, it doesn't matter. The outcome is the same. We'll enjoy each other while she's in town, and then it's finished."

"If you can let a woman like that walk away from you so easily, you really *are* an idiot."

My head comes up in surprise, and Matt's staring at me now, chewing on his food.

"Because I'm not in love with the woman I'm sleeping with? That makes me an idiot? Last time I checked, it made me human. You can't sit there and tell me that you loved every woman you fucked before you met your wife."

His blue eyes narrow, but he doesn't swipe back at me.

"I'm not implying that you have to love all of your sexual partners. Absolutely not. I had my share of fun before I met Nic. I've had experiences that you wouldn't believe."

"What kind of experiences?"

He's quiet for a moment, but he doesn't look around to see if anyone else is listening.

Matt isn't a man to be embarrassed about his life choices.

"I'm a dominant," he says at last. "And I have an affection for bondage."

My jaw wants to drop.

I have a million questions.

"And no, I didn't love every woman I had in my ropes or fucked in the club where I'm a master."

"Jesus, Matt."

"But I knew the minute I saw Nic that she was the only one for me. It's an awareness. A gut feeling that, when you're with her, sexually or not, you can't see yourself doing that with anyone else. And it's not out of regret, but out of contentment."

I take a deep breath, and he continues.

"Not to mention, the thought of another man fucking her the way you do makes you want to kill someone."

My eyes meet his, and he simply grins and nods.

"Yeah, I thought so."

# CHAPTER 9

## SIDNEY

"*S*o, what happens at those guys' parties, anyway?" I ask Keaton as I fold some clothes and stuff them into a small suitcase. "Like, do you get drunk and talk about girls?"

The scowl that immediately comes over his face makes me giggle.

"Fuck no. We eat food and call each other names."

"Sounds like a guy thing." I prop my hands on my hips and examine my progress. I need socks and some pajamas. My favorite hoodie. "But all jokes aside, you had fun?"

"Yeah, it's always a good time when the guys get together. Where are you going?"

I grin over at him and flutter my eyelashes playfully. "I thought you'd never ask. I'm gonna rent a car and drive over to Idaho to see my parents for a few days. I spoke with Maya last night, and she said that Mom's been doing a lot better lately but asked about me yesterday. I'm *right here*, only a six or so-hour drive away. I need to go see them."

"I get that," he says with a nod.

"I should have gone before this. I feel a little guilty about that."

"You're going now," he replies simply.

I've been tempted to ask him to go with me, mostly because I don't love the idea of being away from him, even for a few days.

Which tells me that asking him to go is a bad idea. I *need* to be away from him for a little while. Getting too used to being with him can only spell disaster, with a capital D, in the long run. I'm just setting myself up to have my heart bruised, and that's no one's fault but my own. Keaton has been honest from the beginning.

"I wonder if it's cold there." I frown over at Keaton as I reach for the hoodie. "Do you think it's cold?"

"I'll check the weather app," he replies, pulling his phone out of his pocket and tapping the screen. "Depends on what your definition of cold is because it's gonna be in the sixties, and that doesn't sound too bad to me."

"But their house is on the lake, and it's always a little colder there," I reply, chewing my lip. "I'll take another sweater. How's work going?"

"I'm almost finished with the Mustang, so I'll be passing that on to Uncle Will this week, and then I'll dig into the next thing."

"What's the next thing?"

When he doesn't answer, I turn to look at him. He's sitting in a chair by the window of the main bedroom, his right ankle resting on his left knee, staring at me.

"It's not sexy," he warns me.

"Okay."

"It's a Jeep Wagoneer. From the eighties. It's a commission."

"I don't even know what that is," I admit with a laugh. "But if you say it's not sexy, I believe you."

"It'll be fun, though," he says with a shrug. "It's a big bastard, takes up two bays in the garage, but it's a complete overhaul, so I'm looking forward to the challenge."

"Good, I'm glad you're excited about it. I can't wait to see it."

"Have you been doing any work?"

"I've written a few songs since the party at Leo and Sam's," I admit, feeling the excitement for the music bubble up in my chest. "I think they're good, but who knows if I'll be able to sell them in Nashville."

"Who gives a flying fuck about that?" Keaton says, his voice suddenly hard. "Just *enjoy* it for a change, Sid. Write for the joy of it, not because you're under pressure to sell a hundred million albums."

"Wow, that would be nice." I grin over at him, and when he doesn't smile back, I shrug a shoulder. "Okay, you're right. It's fun to just play with the music, with no pressure to produce something groundbreaking. I really like the piano that I rented. It has a nice sound and fits me well."

I shrug again and turn back to the suitcase. Aside from some toiletries, I think I have everything I need, and if I forget something, I'm sure I can buy it.

"When are you heading out of town?" he asks.

"Tomorrow morning. The rental company is going to drop off the car around eight."

He stands, walks my way, and wraps his arm around my waist.

"Then I want you to stop packing for now because I'm going to get my fill of you to last me for a while."

I feel my eyebrows tip up in surprise as all my nerve endings stand up in awareness. "Is that so?"

"Yeah, that's so." He closes the suitcase and easily lifts it and sets it on the floor next to a dresser I've never used. When he turns back to look at me, his green eyes are full of lust and maybe a little need.

Isn't this what I called and invited him over here for? Because I knew I wouldn't see him for a few days, and I wanted to get my fill of *him* before I left?

His eyes journey from my face, down my chest and the rest of my body, and then slowly make the trip back up to my face.

"That might be the first time in my life that I truly feel like a man just undressed me with his eyes."

"Whether you're dressed or naked, I want you." He takes a step toward me. "You star in every fucking dream at night, and as soon as I'm in a room with you, alone or surrounded by people, I want to touch you. To get you naked and lose myself in you until I don't know where I end and you begin. You fucking undo me, Sidney."

"I had no idea you were so good with words."

He doesn't laugh or even smile. He just continues the slow walk toward me. And when he's within arm's reach, he simply lifts his hand and brushes the tips of his fingers down my cheek.

Just that little touch is enough to send my body into overdrive. My nipples immediately pucker, and my breath catches in my throat.

Everything about this man is pure, unadulterated *sex*.

"I love it when your eyes get heavy like that. It means that you want me, that you're thinking about how I'm going to fuck you, and it turns you the hell on."

"Everything you do turns me on." My voice is thin and breathless, and I can't wait any longer. I reach for him, fist my hands in his shirt, and close the gap between us, pressing my chest to his and boosting up on my toes so I can meet his mouth with mine.

And it's like a switch has been flipped. He's no longer patient. His hands dive under my shirt and brush over my skin, from waist to ribs and over my back.

God, I want to climb him.

It's always like this. The minute we get started with each other, I can't get him or myself naked fast enough.

"Clothes," I mutter against his mouth. "Get them off."

I tug at his shirt, pushing it higher up his torso, until he briefly pulls away from me and yanks it over his head.

And I'm left staring at his smooth chest and ridiculously sculpted abs.

"It's like you were carved out of marble," I mumble as I reach for him. "The ancient Greeks would have worshiped you."

That makes him smirk, but I shake my head.

"It's true. You can laugh all you want, but you're freaking gorgeous."

He slowly shakes his head and reaches for me, gently now that the tempo has slowed just a bit.

With my eyes pinned to his, I reach up and pull the elastic band out of my hair, then shake my head so it falls loose around my shoulders.

Keaton narrows his eyes, and his hands clench into fists at his side.

I pull my top over my head and let it fall, then work on the rest of my clothes. I move efficiently, but I don't hurry because watching Keaton's eyes burn and his jaw clench as I undress is a huge ego booster.

He doesn't have to use words to show me that he thinks I'm attractive.

It's written all over his god-like face.

Once we're both standing here, naked as can be, I reach for him, but he shakes his head.

"Stay like this. Just for a minute." His voice is rough, his eyes hot. "Goddamn, Sid."

I wait, holding my breath, watching emotion roll over his features. Lust, possessiveness, affection, and back to lust again.

"If you don't touch me soon," I warn him, "I'm going to have to start touching myself."

His eyebrows wing up. "Lie on the bed."

He doesn't have to ask me twice. I climb onto the mattress and lie back, expecting him to climb on with me.

Except, he doesn't.

"Spread your legs."

"You can't be serious."

He doesn't respond, simply waits for me to comply. I've had men look at me down there before. Hell, *Keaton* has been down there.

But I've never just spread my legs and put on a show.

"I might be too shy for this." I cringe and cover my face with my hands, totally self-conscious.

"No way, babe." He shakes his head and sits on the end of the bed now, making me feel a little more comfortable, so I spread my fingers to see him. "You're fucking beautiful. You're safe with me."

"I know that."

"If you're uncomfortable, just say so. I don't want

you to do anything that you're not 100 percent okay with, and I mean that."

I relax against the pillows, hands resting on my belly, still watching him.

"You okay?" he asks and reaches out to rub his hand up and down my leg. His touch soothes me.

"Yeah, I'm okay."

"Good girl." He smiles, just the edge of his lips tipping up in that sexy way I love so much. "Will you please open these remarkable legs for me?"

Slowly, I do as he asks, bracing my feet on the covers, knees bent, pussy exposed.

"Jesus Christ, you're beautiful." Those green eyes flick up to mine. "I'd like to watch you touch yourself."

"It's so much better when *you* do the touching."

"I'll reward you with all the touching you can handle."

I bite my lip and, a little self-consciously, let my hand glide down my torso, over my navel, and when I get to my core, I pause.

Keaton licks his lips, but he's not watching my hand at all. He's watching my *face*.

"I want to see what you do to yourself when you think of me."

This isn't what I was expecting *at all*. It makes me a little bolder, and my fingers drift down, into my already wet folds, over my hard clit.

I inhale sharply, and his eyes narrow.

I moan, and he swears under his breath.

134

I close my eyes, and I'm suddenly under him, his lips pressed to mine, his hand over my own as he guides my fingers through me, over me, *in* me.

"So much better," I moan against his lips, and mentally beg him not to stop the magic he's doing with his hand over mine.

Finally, he guides my hand up to his lips, pulls my wet finger into his mouth, and sucks on it.

"Need you," I whisper as he lowers his forehead to my own. "Never stops."

"Shit, baby."

I hear the packet opening, and then he's in me, seated fully and struggling to catch his breath.

His hips begin to move in tandem with mine as I wrap my legs around him, and I know without a shadow of a doubt that we're chasing the same release.

I grip his ass in my hands, not afraid to let my nails dig into his flesh.

When the orgasm consumes me, I cry out, holding on for dear life as wave after wave crashes over me.

And then he's with me, shuddering with his own release.

It's in this moment that I know, deep down, that I've fallen completely in love with Keaton Williams, even though I also know that it's a mistake. He's made it clear that he won't ever love me back.

But I can't help myself. It's completely out of my control, and I know I'm going to get hurt because of it.

~

IT'S STILL dark outside when I wake. When I reach over to Keaton's side of the bed, the sheets are cool, and he's gone.

But I can hear the music.

I climb out of bed, pull his T-shirt over my head, and tug on a clean pair of panties before padding out into the living room, where Keaton's seated on the piano bench, playing a song that I swear I know, but I can't put my finger on it.

He's only in jeans, and his bare foot presses on the pedal as he plays.

It could be the sexiest thing I've ever seen, this amazing man seated here in the dark, playing a beautiful melody.

"You can sit," he says softly.

Not willing to pass on that invitation, I sit next to him on the bench as he scoots to make room for me, and I lean my head on his bare shoulder as he continues to play.

"What is it?" I ask.

"'Unchained Melody,'" he says in a soft voice.

"That's it," I say with a sigh. "God, I love this song."

He doesn't reply; he just keeps playing so perfectly that it brings tears to my eyes.

So, I close them and don't even swipe at the tears that roll down my cheeks. I'm soaking in the music, every beautiful note as he serenades me here in the dark. When he reaches the bridge, the intensity of each note leaves me breathless. The end of the song softens, the crescendo dissipates, and with the last note, Keaton lifts his hands from the keys and rests them on his thighs.

"Wow." I wipe at the tears now, and he turns to kiss the crown of my head. "You're so talented, Keaton."

"Hmm."

"Keep playing. Please?"

"You have a long drive today," he whispers, his lips still pressed to my hair. "You should be sleeping."

"I'd rather listen to you. I can sleep when I get there."

He doesn't move right away, but then he shifts, and notes fill the air once more. This one I recognize immediately.

Without even knowing it, he's playing a song that's so appropriate for this moment, because I *can't* help falling in love with him.

Music always makes me emotional. It goes with the territory of being a musician. But this one has me all up in my feelings.

I'm content to sit here, next to this fascinating, sexy man, and listen to him play an instrument that I love so much. I'd sit here with him forever if it were possible.

But soon, the moment is over, and Keaton wraps his arm around my shoulders.

"You really should get some more sleep."

"Come back to bed with me."

He stands, holds his hand out for mine, and leads me to the bedroom.

～

"You're here!" Maya jogs down to the car to greet me, throws her arms around me, and hugs me close. "I didn't think you'd *ever* drive up."

"Did you tell the parents that I was coming?"

"Nope, your secret is safe with me. They're going to be so excited to see you." My older sister grins and takes one of my bags to carry for me, her steps light and bouncy beside me.

Maya is shorter than me, with dark hair and the bluest eyes ever, but no one would ever mistake that we weren't sisters.

We share the same laugh and the same eye shape.

She's one of my favorite people in the world, and I've always looked up to her.

"How have things been here?" I ask as we climb the steps of our childhood home.

"Not bad, actually. The new medication that Mom's trying is working wonders. She's so much better with it, hasn't fallen, and seems to be more herself lately."

"That's the best news ever. Where are they?"

"Dad took Mom to a checkup. They should be back in the next hour or so."

"Perfect. That gives me time to unpack and chat with my favorite sister."

"What a coincidence," she says as we climb the steps to the second floor, where our bedrooms are. "You're *my* favorite sister."

It's the same banter we've had since we were kids, and it makes us both smile since we're each other's *only* sisters.

"Want me to get you something to drink while you unpack?" she asks.

"Absolutely not. I want you to stay here and talk to me, and then we'll go down and get something together."

"Good. I wanted to lie on the bed and be lazy all along," Maya says with a laugh and jumps onto the bed and cradles a pillow to her chest while I unzip a bag and dig in.

It feels good to stand after being in the car for so long today. But every mile, every minute of the drive, was well worth it.

"How are things in Seattle?" Maya asks when I return from the bathroom, where I just stowed my toiletries.

"It's good. The weather's been nice. Gray and Stella are disgustingly happy. Seriously, it's kind of gross, the way they paw at each other all the time."

Maya wrinkles her nose.

"But the Montgomery family is super nice."

"Yeah, I was surprised at how welcoming they were when we went to the wedding last year."

"It wasn't an act, I can tell you that. They've

included me in a bunch of stuff, including a family party that Leo Nash hosted *at his house.*"

Her eyes almost bug out of her head. "You're kidding me."

"I'm not. And then, I got to go up to Leo's studio and jam with him *and* write a freaking *song* with him."

"Stop it."

"I can't. Because *then*, we put on a little show for the whole family, which is freaking huge. We played some of my songs and some of Leo's songs. Hell, we even played some of Brax's songs and a few of Starla's, too."

"*Starla* was there?"

"No. She was in LA, but apparently, she's related to them somehow or other, and she's usually at these parties when she's in town."

"This is crazy," Maya mutters, shaking her head.

"I kept thinking about you, wishing you were there because you would have loved it. But you'll go to the next one."

Her eyes fill with sadness, and I frown at her.

"What's wrong?"

"I don't go anywhere these days, Sid."

"But you said that the medication is working, so hopefully that means you'll have a little more freedom now."

"Maybe." She bites her lip, and tears fill her eyes, and I immediately abandon my suitcase and sit next to her, pulling her hands into mine. "I feel like such an asshole for getting upset."

"You're not an asshole. Don't talk about my sister like that. What's wrong?"

"I love Mom, you know I do."

"I know." And I can already see where this is going. "But you're not a caregiver, Maya. You're not trained to be an in-home nurse."

"No, but damn it, she's my *mom*. I should be able to do this. I *am* doing it."

"You're doing an awesome job," I assure her. "Anytime I speak with Mom or Dad on the phone, they can't say enough about you."

"It's just hard," Maya says with a sigh and wipes her tears. "I feel like she's turned a corner, and she has more good days than bad ones now, but the bad ones suck, you know?"

"I know, and I feel like a complete jerk for leaving you here to do this all yourself. Maybe I should let the condo in Seattle go and find a place here. I can write music and take the sabbatical here at home so I can take some of this off your plate."

"You don't have to do that," she assures me. "Absolutely not. I know you're getting some actual rest out there and enjoying yourself for the first time in a *long* time."

"Yeah, while you're here with all this responsibility heaped on your shoulders. Talk about unfair."

She nibbles on her bottom lip. "Maybe you could just come over here more often. Like every other weekend or something."

"We can work that out," I assure her and pull her in for a big hug. I hate that she clings just a little too hard, telling me exactly how stressed out she's been here. "And I'll talk to Mom and Dad, too. We need to do what's best for everyone, M."

She sighs and pulls back, wiping her wet cheeks. "I know. We'll figure it out. Anyway, I'm so glad you're here. Now, finish putting that stuff away so we can go down and sit on the deck and watch the water. It's super nice out today."

"I THINK I just heard them drive up," I say, thirty minutes later. Maya and I grabbed some iced coffees, and we've been sitting out on the deck that faces the lake, soaking in the late spring sunshine and watching the brave souls who couldn't resist taking their boats out on the water.

Sure, it's sunny, but it's still cold for boating.

"I heard it, too," Maya agrees. "They'll see us out here."

I'm excited to see their faces when they realize that I'm out here.

It doesn't take long for the back door to open, and when I turn to see who it is, I grin at my mom, who's stopped short, staring at me in shock.

"Why, Sidney." She rushes forward, and I meet her halfway, wrapping my arms around her and holding on. "Oh, baby girl, we didn't know you were coming home."

"I know. I made Maya keep it a secret." I kiss her cheek and then pull back so I can see her. She looks so much better than she did last year. Her eyes are clear, and she doesn't look nearly as fragile as before. "You look amazing, Mom."

"Sid?"

I turn and smile at Dad, who looks just as surprised as Mom.

"Hi, Daddy."

He joins us in a group hug, and before I know it, Maya has looped her arms around all of us.

"I love sappy moments," Maya says, making us all laugh.

"When did you arrive?" Mom asks as we sit next to each other and continue holding hands.

"Just about an hour ago," I reply and take a deep breath of fresh mountain air. "I drove over from Seattle this morning."

"That's the strange car in the driveway," Dad says with a nod.

We spend some time catching up on my time in Seattle, and then I turn to face Mom and Dad, who's sitting on the other side of her.

"How are you feeling? *Really*. I'm not far away and on the phone. I need to know how things really are here."

Mom smiles softly and pats my hand. "I'm *really* doing better."

"She is," Dad confirms, immediately slipping into his doctor's voice. "She's responding very well to the new medication. Better than her doctors anticipated, in fact. From what we're seeing, and the research still being done, your mother should be able to be on this medication for the rest of her life, and it *should* continue to help. We don't know what it'll look like twenty years from now, but for right now, she's stabilized."

It used to amuse me how Dad sounds when he's wearing his doctor hat. He's a well-respected cardiologist. Now, his voice simply soothes me.

"No confusion?" I ask her.

"No, I haven't had any significant symptoms in a couple of months now."

I feel Maya shift behind me, so I turn and address her.

"What? You're with her every day. Do you not agree with her?"

With all eyes on my older sister, she shifts again, looking uncertain.

"It's okay, honey," Mom assures her. "Have you noticed something?"

"I agree that there are *way* more good days than bad," Maya confirms, "but there are still times that you seem a little unsteady. You're not as forgetful, but when you get tired or overwhelmed, you need a break."

"I think that's pretty normal, and expected," Dad replies with a nod. "It could take six months before we see all the effects of the medication. But the fact that she's made the gains she has in such a short time is very encouraging."

"I agree," Maya agrees quickly. "And I'm not discounting it at all. I love that it feels like I have my mom back, the way she's always been."

"Oh, sweet girl," Mom says and smiles over at Maya. "Let me tell you, *I* like having myself back, too. It's a confusing disease, and I've been worried about all of you. I feel a lot better, and we have every reason to believe that it will get even better from here."

"I'm so glad." I lean over and kiss her cheek. "I just want you to feel healthy."

"That's always the goal," Dad says with a nod. "I'm not her physician, but I'm very pleased with the progress."

"That's high praise, coming from him," Mom says with a grin. "Now, how long are you here, and what are we going to do with our time? I don't get to spend time with my baby often enough."

"I'm here for a few days, and I want to eat and chat, and maybe we can all go to the spa or do something fun. Dad, are you on at the hospital?"

"Only tomorrow," he says with a wink. "I'll be around. You ladies should go get pampered at the spa, on me."

"I won't turn that down," Maya says, clapping her hands. "Thanks, Dad."

~

I'VE ALWAYS SPENT a lot of time outside, looking at the water. I used to bring my guitar out here, as I have now, to play and let the music get lost in the breeze.

It energizes me.

And when I was little, the house was always busy, full of Maya's and Gray's friends. Although, I'm a lot younger than Gray, so by the time I was old enough to annoy him, he was off to college.

Maya, however, had to deal with me being underfoot, trying to hang out with her friends.

Annoying the hell out of her.

And when the house got too busy or loud, and I was told yet again to go find something else to do, I'd come out here and play. Before I knew how to play the guitar, I'd hum and sing.

After high school, I knew I didn't want to go to college. I wanted to make music.

So, much to my parents' dismay, I packed up and went to Nashville. Less than a year later, I had a contract with a major label, and I was living the dream.

I always come home to visit, because I love my family so much, but I've never really looked back or ever considered moving home.

There hasn't been time.

"How bad is it?"

Without a pause in the song I'm playing on the strings, I turn and see Maya standing behind me. The sun is just starting to set, and it's getting colder outside.

She has her arms full of hoodies and blankets.

"How bad is what?" I ask as I set the guitar aside and accept the sweater and a blanket. Maya settles into the chair next to mine, pulls her legs up to her chest, and watches me with her pretty blue eyes.

"When you called to tell us that you were going to Seattle, you said it was because you needed a vacation and that you'd fill us in on the rest later. It's later, Sid. What's up?"

I blow out a breath and glance over in time to see an eagle soar silently over the water, then scoop up a fish for his dinner.

And I fill her in. From the dismal record and tour sales, to coming home to find Annie in my house, and also my time in Seattle.

I tell her everything, even about my relationship with Keaton.

And it feels so *good* to confide in my big sister.

"You'll get another contract," she says, waving that part off. "You're too good, and you have a huge following, Sid. Your career will survive this."

"I'm so glad you're sure of that, because I'm not."

"It's scary," she agrees with a nod. "And it's always a hit to the ego to be told that you're no longer wanted. It's like a bad breakup."

"Yes, that's exactly it." I nod, then tip my head back against the chair and look up at the stars beginning to come out. "It absolutely was a hit to my ego. I've worked my ass off since I was seventeen. I graduated early, remember?"

"Of course, I remember. I thought Mom was going to have a stroke at the thought of you driving out to Nashville and making a go of it by yourself. But you've always been so sure and so strong that we knew you'd do well."

"I'm sure they worried about me." I bite my lower lip and look over at my sister. "Is it possible that my career is already over? It feels like I just got it in my grasp."

"No." She shakes her head, leaving no room for argument. "Don't forget that you've made a lot of friends in the industry. You've sung with superstars, honey. You start making calls. Maybe you can do a duet album or, hell, I don't know. Something."

"That could be fun." I tap my lips with my finger. "Leo said that if I ever needed anything, I could reach out to him."

"Ask him for advice," she says. "He's been in this business forever. He'll have thoughts on it. Also? You don't use social media enough."

"I hate it." I stick out my lower lip in a pout. "I know it's highly unusual for people my age to dislike social media since that's what we grew up on, but I really do hate it."

"You don't have to love it to *use* it," she advises me. "Get your fans excited to see you. Have you heard from Annie yet?"

"Not really. She said she'd set me up with some interviews and stuff, but she's been quiet. I've only been out west for a couple of weeks. Maybe she's still trying to give me a break."

"Maybe. But that doesn't mean you can't start doing some stuff on your own. Get on the apps and *sing*. Your fans will love it."

"Ugh."

Maya laughs and reaches out with a foot to kick me gently on the knee.

"You can do it. You're charismatic, beautiful, and have the voice of an angel. You've got this."

"You know, I don't think I realized how much I needed this pep talk until just now."

"That's what big sisters are for." She smiles over at me, and it feels like it did when we were young, and I needed to lean on her for advice and help.

"I don't think I want to live in Nashville full time anymore, M."

That makes her eyes widen.

"I'm telling you, this will blow over," she insists.

"That's not it."

"Don't give up your life in Nashville for a man who's made it plain as day that he won't commit to you, Sid. Don't be that girl."

"I'm *not* that girl." I shake my head and laugh. "No, I

just miss the mountains and the Pacific Northwest in general. Plus, I should be closer so I can help out here."

"Let's not talk about that tonight," Maya says. "Let's have a fun few days together and get a plan for you to conquer the country music world, and then we'll figure out the rest."

"Yeah, okay." I blow out a breath and snuggle down deeper into the blanket. "It gets cold fast here."

"Hell yes, it does. Why are we outside?"

I laugh and stand to gather my things. "Let's go see if Mom and Dad want to watch a movie."

"I'll pop the popcorn."

# CHAPTER 10

## KEATON

*S*idney's been gone for forty-eight hours, and all I've done is bury myself in work. Which is exactly what I did before she walked back into my life less than a month ago.

But now it just feels so…pathetic.

"Knock, knock."

I poke my head out of the engine of the Jeep that I finally started and see my mom walking into my shop.

"You don't usually come out here," I say as I reach for the rag to wipe off my hands. She's carrying a soft-sided cooler as she walks over to me and leans in to kiss my cheek. "I would hug you, but I don't want to mess you up. I'm covered in grease."

"You have a messy job," she replies with a grin. "I brought you lunch. Mostly, I was just missing you today and wanted to come see you."

"That's actually really sweet. Want to take this into the house?"

"No, because if I go in there, I'll want to decorate everything, and you won't let me, so let's just keep this nice visit out here, where I'm fully out of my element. You know," she continues as she wanders around, taking everything in, "I might have to come back here with my camera. Take some photos. You could put them on your website."

"I don't have a website."

She shakes her head at me. "You need one."

"For what? I have more work than I can handle."

"Still. You should show off your work and share all your blood, sweat, and tears with the world. Maybe you could use the photos for social media."

"I don't have—"

"Social media," she finishes for me. "Yeah, I know. One of your sisters would probably do it for you."

I open the cooler and pull out one of the three sandwiches inside and take a bite. "This is delicious. Thanks, I was hungry."

"You're welcome. Have you seen Sidney lately?"

"And now we know why you're *really* here." I take another bite as Mom cringes, then shrugs.

"I'm your mother. I want to know these things. So sue me."

"What do you want to know?"

"Everything except the sex," she immediately replies. "Not that I'm a prude, but thinking about my children having sex doesn't exactly sit well with me."

I pop the rest of the sandwich into my mouth and reach for another.

"I don't think I want to discuss my sex life with my mom anyway."

She grins and reaches into the bag for one of three pouches of chips and digs in. "So, how is she?"

"Who?"

Mom narrows her eyes on me and shoves another chip into her mouth. "You know, you *used* to be my favorite son."

"I'm your only son."

She just holds her eyes on mine, the same green as my own, and waits.

Natalie Williams is *ruthless* when it comes to getting information out of her kids. She doesn't nag; she just waits. Patiently.

Too patiently.

Until we cave.

"She's fine," I finally reply and reach for my own chips. "She's in Idaho this week, visiting her family."

"Oh, how nice. How is her mom feeling?"

"Better, I guess. Sidney seemed happy with everything when I spoke with her the other night."

"I'm so glad. I really enjoyed her parents when we met them at Liv and Vaughn's wedding. When is she coming back to Seattle?"

"I'm not sure. She's playing it by ear."

"Well, I'm sure they're all enjoying each other. I'm surprised Stella and Gray didn't drive over to join them."

"I think they had a lot of work and couldn't get away."

She nods thoughtfully. "Are you in love with her?"

"Stella? She's my *cousin*. I don't think that would be a good idea."

"You always were the smart-ass in the family," she says and wipes her hands on her jeans. "Sidney, of course. Are you in love with her?"

"No."

It's a bald-faced lie, and we both know it. I can see in her eyes that she doesn't believe me.

"I don't know why not. She's beautiful, talented, and smart. If that's not good enough for you, your standards might be just a smidge too high, honey."

"I never said she's not good enough for me." I pretend to check the time on my imaginary watch. "Well, look at the time. I'd better get back to work."

"Smart-ass," she says again. "I'm just trying to have an honest conversation here."

"You're prying," I counter. "And sure, I know it's because you love me, but you're also my mom, and you're nosy as hell."

"I am, too," she says, feigning indignation. "Do you at least *like* her?"

"Of course, I do."

"But you don't *love* her."

I don't say this out loud, but I *can't* love Sidney. Our lifestyles will never mesh, and I've been honest with both of us from the start.

"Mom, I love you."

"I love you, too, baby."

"And I love seeing you. Thank you for the lunch and for coming to visit."

"It's my pleasure. Is this your way of telling me that it's none of my business and I've worn out my welcome?"

"Yes."

Mom laughs and walks over to kiss me on the cheek again. "Okay, point taken. I *do* love you very much, and I like Sidney. When we saw you two together at Leo's party, you looked so happy together, and don't think I didn't notice that you were holding her hand."

"She was nervous."

"I don't buy that that's the only reason you didn't leave her side all day." She shakes her head and turns to leave. "But I'm just your mom. What do I know, anyway?"

"Pack your bags. We're going on a guilt trip."

That makes her laugh again. "If you ever want to talk about it, or anything at all, you know where to find me."

"I know." I kick the tire of the Jeep and sigh. "Sorry, Mom. I'm not trying to be a jerk. I just don't really have much to report that isn't sex."

She scrunches up her nose and then grins. "Have fun. Be safe. Although, I wouldn't mind being a grandma sooner or later."

"Not from me, not any time soon."

She waves and walks out of the shop, headed toward her little Lexus.

I adore my mom. As far as I'm concerned, that woman hung the fucking moon, and I've always been able to talk just about anything through with her.

But I don't have anything worked out in my head where Sidney is concerned. I crave her. I *need* to be around her, to touch her and talk with her. Make her laugh.

Everything about her is a turn-on, physically and mentally.

And if I dig deep enough, I could likely see that I've fallen for her.

But I can't go down that road. It's not fair to either of us.

I zip up the cooler, saving the rest of the food for later, and turn back to the Jeep. I have to dig into work and focus my energy on that, my family, and things that I can commit to.

After a few minutes, I swear, then wipe my hands off once again and reach for my phone.

I want to hear Sidney's voice.

So, I dial her number and wait until she answers.

"Hey there, handsomest guy I've ever seen," she says, her voice bright and full of excitement.

"Hey, back at you. What has you so excited?"

"I literally *just* hung up the phone with my agent, Annie. She was calling to let me know that I have an interview with *Music Row*, only one of the hottest magazines focused on country music, and that's not even the best news!" I can hear her jumping up and down through the phone.

"Tell me the best part."

"Holy fucking shit, I haven't even told my parents yet. They're going to *freak* out."

"You're killing me here, sweetheart."

"Okay. I have to breathe." She takes a deep breath in and out. "I've been invited to the Grand Ole Opry to help induct Misty McIntyre as a member. Holy shit, Keaton, it's such an honor! Misty and I have been through the country trenches together for *years*. We've played the Opry together, and I just couldn't be more thrilled for her. And she's asked that I be one of the musicians who perform and celebrate with her."

"That's *awesome*, babe."

"It's so amazing," she continues. "I don't think I'd be more excited if *I* was the one being inducted. Misty's the best there is, and I love that she wants me there. Holy shit, what am I going to wear?"

"I know you'll figure out the wardrobe," I reply with a smile.

"You have to go with me."

I swear my heart stops beating. "What?"

"You *have* to," she continues. "I need a date, and

you're my date. We're not seeing other people, remember?"

"Well, yeah, but—"

"Oh, I can't wait to introduce you to so many people. They're all so nice. And the people who work at the Opry are all just the *best.* They host an amazing party for the inductee, friends, and industry people, and the show is *so* great. I promise you'll have fun, and you'll get to see where I live, too. My house isn't big, but it's pretty, and oh! I can introduce you to Wendy—"

"No."

"I can ask the press to—what do you mean, no?"

"Exactly what I said. Absolutely not."

"Keaton," she says, some of the air coming out of her sails, and I feel like a dick. "This is really important to me."

"I've never lied to you," I reply, my voice firm. "I don't do public appearances. I'm not your date for anything like that, Sid. You *know* that."

"But...this is different."

"It's not different. Listen, I'm excited for you, and I'm proud of you. You'll knock it out of the park. I hope you have an amazing time, but I'm not going with you. That's not the deal."

"Right. Of course. What was I thinking? I have to go celebrate with people who love me now." Her voice is hollow, and I curse under my breath. "Have a good day, Keaton."

She hangs up, and I want to throw my phone across the garage.

"Goddamn it," I snarl and pace in a circle before taking a deep breath that does nothing to calm me down.

It's better this way. No strings, that's what we said. No rules. The only rule was that we were monogamous for however long it lasted.

I held up that side of the bargain.

"Then why do I feel like an ass?"

"WHAT ARE YOU DOING HERE?" Olivia asks me, two days later. I'm sitting by the pool at her house, talking with Vaughn.

"I invited him over," Vaughn replies to his wife. "We're talking about cars."

"Oh, is there one you want Keaton to work on for you?"

"Yep, and I've almost got him talked into it." Vaughn stands and walks over to my sister, wraps his arm around her waist, and pulls her in for a kiss. "Where are you off to?"

"Shopping with Stella and Sidney."

My head whips up from my phone. "Sidney?"

Liv frowns. "Yeah, didn't you know she's back in town? We have to go find a *spectacular* dress for her to wear to some pretty important shindig in Nashville

KRISTEN PROBY

later this week. We're always happy to help a woman in fashion need."

"You're so selfless," Vaughn says, nuzzling her neck. "Let's order takeout later, just you and me."

"It's a date." She grins and frames his face, pulling him in for a kiss.

"Gross," I mutter with a sigh, which only makes the two of them grin and keep kissing.

Finally, they pull apart, and Liv waves. "See you later."

"See you," I reply as Vaughn returns to his seat across from me. "Did you know Sid was back?"

"I would have no reason to know that," he replies easily. "The interesting thing is, *you* didn't know."

I shake my head, ready to change the subject already.

"Let's talk about the car. I think you should go with the '66 Charger. It was the first year it was made, and it's a sweetheart of a car."

"Okay, I'm good with that. How long do you think it'll take you to find one?" Vaughn asks.

"Hard to say. I'll start putting out the word that I'm looking for one. Could take a few weeks, could be a year. I couldn't get it on the calendar until this winter, though, even for family."

Vaughn grins. "That's pretty fucking awesome, man. Good for you."

"Thanks. We'll start talking specifics once I find the

vehicle for you. You can have any paint color, leather, you name it."

"I'm looking forward to it. Out of curiosity, what's the cost?"

I blow out a breath, thinking it over. "It'll probably be a couple thousand for the car, depending on the condition. Then, you add in materials, engine, transmission, paint, and leather..." I tip my head from side to side. "Probably about a buck fifty."

Vaughn's eyebrow lifts. "A hundred and fifty thousand dollars?"

"Give or take. That's the family discount. It might not be that much."

"Damn, Keaton, you're running one hell of a business."

"What do you bring in per film these days?"

Now my brother-in-law grins across from me. "It varies, but averages somewhere around eight to ten million."

I knew that. "Hell of a business."

"Touché." Vaughn holds his beer up to clink it to mine. "Your sister is fucking proud of you."

"Big sisters are supposed to be proud. I could be flipping burgers somewhere, and she'd still be proud. Not that there's anything wrong with flipping burgers. I *like* a good cheeseburger."

"I hear that. And yeah, that's true. She'd be proud either way, but she gets excited when the family talks about your business. It's cool to watch."

161

"Liv is the best there is, even if she is a pain in my ass half the time." I take a swig of beer. "I'll keep you posted on the Charger. It'll be a sweet ride when I'm done with it."

"Do that. I'm excited about getting started, but I also respect your schedule. There's no rush. Do you mind if I swing by once in a while to watch once you get started on her?"

"I don't mind. I might put you to work."

"That doesn't bother me."

He walks me to the door and shakes my hand when I'm on the way out.

"Tell Sidney I said hi when you manage to track her down." His grin is smug.

"Who said I was going to do that?"

He just laughs and closes the door in my face.

I jump into the Bronco and start it up, then push my hands through my hair.

Yeah, I'll go find Sid later tonight and get things straightened out.

SHE HASN'T CALLED or texted me. Obviously, she's pissed, and I get it, but she's back in Seattle, and she hasn't said a word to me. Nothing.

The shopping spree has to be long over, so I pull into her parking spot in the underground garage and take the elevator up to her floor.

I could have texted to let her know that I'm on my way, but that would only give her an opportunity to shut me down, and I *will* get this cleared up with her. Now that we're both calm, we can have a conversation about the whole situation. I can apologize, and we can just move the hell on. I missed her over the past few days, and I need to get my hands on her.

I ring her doorbell and rock back on my heels, push my hands into my pockets, and hope that she doesn't slam the door in my face.

Finally, the door opens, and Sid's expression goes from curiosity to complete annoyance in the blink of an eye. She starts to push the door closed, but I plant my hand on it, stopping her.

"Go away, Keaton."

"No, damn it. Let me in so I can talk to you."

"Not much to say," she points out, but steps away from the door and simply walks across the room, away from me, her ass swaying in little yoga shorts and those spectacular legs on full display.

I close the door and watch as she opens her fridge and pulls out a bottle of water, cracks it open, and takes a sip, her eyes on me.

"I'm listening. Say what you need to say and then get the hell out of here." Her blue eyes spark with annoyance.

It's worse than I thought.

"I didn't mean to sound like such an asshole the other day. I honestly didn't. I'm excited for you to go to

163

the show and celebrate with your friends. You deserve to share in that, and I know that you're excited about it, too."

"How nice of you."

I clench my teeth and ball my hands. "I told you early on, I don't do the spotlight, Sidney. Call it anxiety or stubbornness or whatever, but it doesn't change how I feel about it."

"I wasn't asking you to 'do the spotlight', as you put it."

"You know as well as I do that the press is going to be crawling all over the place at that event."

"Yeah, but—"

"And you know that I don't do that shit. I want *nothing* to do with it, ever. Not even for you."

"You've made that abundantly clear, Keaton. You didn't have to come all this way to drive it home for me. I'm not an idiot; I understand what you're saying. Now, you can leave the way you came, and don't let the door hit you on the ass on the way out. I have to pack."

"You're leaving again." It's not a question.

"For fuck's sake, I'm going to *Nashville*. Like I told you. The show is this weekend, so I need to get back."

This is it. She's leaving. I had less than a month with her, and I royally fucked it up.

"Are you coming back?"

"Sooner or later," is all she says as she rubs her face with the heels of her hands.

"Sidney." I walk toward her, but she holds her hands up, stopping me.

"If you think I want you to touch me right now, you're not reading the room very well. You're not exactly welcome here tonight, Keaton."

"I'm sorry." I stop at the other side of the kitchen island, itching to get my hands on her. "I'm *sorry*. If tonight is your last night in Seattle—"

She laughs now and shakes her head. "You have a lot of nerve. You think that because I'm leaving I want to fuck you? After the way you've made me feel? Not a chance. You know the way out."

She walks away, down the hall to her bedroom, without giving me a backward glance, and there's absolutely nothing I can do about it.

"Bye, Sid."

# CHAPTER 11

## SIDNEY

"*H*ow are you, Wendy?" The older woman is helping me organize everything in my closet that I'll need for my performance.. I have a whole glam squad coming tomorrow at noon to help me get ready for Misty's big celebration at the Opry, and there's also a lot of prep work involved beforehand.

Wendy's a lifesaver.

"Oh, I'm just fine," she says with a smile. I've always thought of Wendy as my Nashville mom. She's so nurturing, always ready to jump in and help me in any way that I might need. "I admit, I miss seeing you. You were on tour and then immediately took off to have some adventures in Seattle."

"Yeah, I haven't been home much." I sigh and look around. It's all so familiar, and yet, I don't know if it really is *home* anymore. "I was excited to get this opportunity to come back to town for some work, if I'm being honest."

"You didn't even take a full month off," she reminds me.

"I know, but I like to work. I've been doing some writing while in Seattle. I have about eight songs written or partially written. They just need to be polished up."

"Well, that has to be a good feeling." Wendy takes the dress I bought, with Olivia's and Stella's help, out of the garment bag, and her eyes almost bug out of her head. "Wow."

"I can't wait to wear it," I confess with a grin.

"Where's the other half of it?" She pretends to look around for a skirt, and it makes me giggle. "Then again, if anyone has the legs for this thing, it's you, Sid."

"Thanks." I know that my legs are part of my image. They always have been. I perform in short skirts and short shorts, and I *always* wear stiletto heels to accentuate my leg muscles. I work out often, keeping my legs in shape. "But the upper part is all covered up. It even has long sleeves."

The dress is by Valentino. It's blush pink, with sequins all over it, making it shimmer in the light. It has long sleeves and a high neck, completely covering my chest.

"Sure, but no back to speak of."

"Okay, I'm going to show a lot of skin." I shrug and admire the dress on the hanger.

"Do it while you're young," Wendy advises with a wink. "You'll look spectacular in this. I assume you bought new shoes, too?"

"Of course." I reach for the box of sparkly Jimmy Choos that match the dress and grin. "They'll kill my feet, but they'll be pretty."

Wendy laughs and sets them on my shelf for me.

"I must admit, Seattle looks good on you, kiddo."

My eyes whip over to her in surprise. "What do you mean?"

"You're happy. You have a bit of a glow to you, one that I haven't seen in a while. I know that touring is exhausting, but it wasn't just that I saw before you left for the west coast."

"I did have a good time out west. It was nice to spend time with my brother and his fiancée, and then I spent a few days with my parents and Maya. It really helped to fill my cup back up, as my mom would say."

"No man?"

My hands still at Wendy's question, and then I shrug my shoulder. "Yeah, there's a guy out there. But it's definitely nothing serious."

"Well, it was good for you, then. Will you stay in Nashville now or go back to Seattle?"

"I haven't decided," I reply honestly. "I didn't let the condo go yet, in case I want to go back, but I brought all my things home with me. Tomorrow night might be a deciding factor, depending on how I'm welcomed.

Country music is a small family, and sometimes I feel like I'm on the outside, looking in."

"I hope that you find what you need tomorrow night. My husband and I are going to the show. We scored some tickets."

"Oh, that's so exciting. I love watching shows at the Opry. It's just so...*country*."

Wendy grins, and with everything situated for now, we walk down to the kitchen.

"Are you *sure* you don't want me to come in the morning and help out with anything?" she asks.

"No, it should be just fine. You enjoy the day, and I'll see you tomorrow night at the show. I'm going with Rick Collins."

Her eyebrows both fly up at that.

"He's the hottest thing in country music right now. Good for you, honey."

"We're *friends*," I reply. "We've known each other a long time, and neither of us wanted to go alone. He's performing, too."

"Still, he'll look damn good on your arm, and vice versa." Wendy winks and grabs her purse. "Give me a buzz in the morning if you need me."

"You're a mother hen, you know that?"

"It's just in my DNA," she says with a laugh. "Welcome home."

She waves and then walks out the back door to her car.

I take a deep breath and turn to look at my kitchen.

It's bright, with white cabinets and marble countertops, and I absolutely *adore* the deep farmhouse sink that I just had to have when we remodeled the space. I love this kitchen.

I've never cooked a meal in it, but I love it.

And now that I'm back, and walking through my house, I can admit that I really like this house. As I told Keaton, it's not huge, but it's cozy, updated, and decorated just the way I like it.

But it feels empty. And lonely.

And I don't know if I've ever felt that before, being in this house.

"You're moping," I mutter to myself. "Keaton hurt your feelings, and you're pouting over it. Stop that. It's not sexy, and it's totally annoying."

I open the freezer and retrieve a pint of ice cream, open the lid, and grab a spoon.

Maybe this will help me forget about Keaton Williams.

"You know, it's not polite to upstage the inductee," Rick says with a grin when he walks into my house the next afternoon to pick me up. "You're hot as hell, Sidney."

"You're sweet." I do a little twirl and bask in Rick's whistle. Yeah, I look hot in this dress, and the shoes tie it all together. "I might keep this one for a tour. It would need some modifications, and tights would be a must, but it's a good one."

"No one's going to be looking at Misty with you in that dress."

I roll my eyes at him. "Trust me, her dress is hot as hell, too. She sent me a picture a few days ago."

Rick doesn't look bad himself. He's tall, with light blond hair and brown eyes, and he has a smile that would make a woman's panties melt off at fifty paces.

Tonight, he's rocking some scruff on his cheeks and a blue suit with a T-shirt under it.

No tie.

Somehow, Rick's able to pull off the look effortlessly.

"What songs are you singing?" I ask him as I check my makeup one last time in the hall mirror. "I had a hard time choosing from Misty's catalog. She has too many good ones."

"We had to choose from *Misty's* catalog?"

I glance over, and he looks shocked, then grins once more.

"Kidding. I wanted to do 'Moonshine'."

"Oh, that would make an awesome duet," I reply with a nod. "Good choice. We're doing 'Girls Gone Bad'. Because we're sassy."

Rick laughs and escorts me out to the waiting car.

The drive into the city and to the Opry House takes about thirty minutes, and when we pull up, I take a long, deep breath.

The press is already out front, waiting to take photos of all of us on the red carpet.

"Ready for this show?" Rick asks me.

"As I'll ever be."

The door opens, and Rick exits first, then turns back to offer me his hand. I take it, and we turn to the cameras, already smiling.

"Sidney! Over here!"

"Rick! Give us a smolder!"

"What the hell is a smolder?" I ask Rick under my breath.

"Look at me."

I comply, and he's staring down at me with intense brown eyes, no smile anywhere on his face.

"Is that the smolder?"

"Yes, ma'am."

I nod. "I get it."

With a laugh, Rick leads me slowly down the carpet, where we're photographed and interviewed.

"Are you two an item?" someone calls out.

"We're friends," I reply. "We've known each other for a long time, and Rick was nice enough to escort me this evening."

Finally, we move into the building and get a break from the flashes.

"Nicely done," Rick says and kisses my hand before letting me go. "Now, let's go get our grub on."

"I don't think I can eat anything in this dress," I admit.

∽

THE OPRY INDUCTEE parties are legendary. The staff makes sure that there is always a signature cocktail and food that is all requested by the artist being honored.

Misty's cocktail is a Misty Martini, of course, and there's lots of pizza spread out, with a million different topping combinations for everyone to enjoy.

As the show goes on, people come in and out of the party room to watch on the screens and eat and chat.

I used to get so starstruck when people like Garth and Trisha would come to the shows, but now it's like I'm part of a really cool club, and we're getting together to celebrate someone we love.

Because at the base of it, that's exactly what this is.

And it absolutely tears my heart out that I might not be able to do this for much longer.

"Why are you so mopey?" Annie asks as she joins me, cocktail in hand.

"I'm not. I'm having a great time." I glance at the monitor where Misty and Rick are currently singing. "Their harmonies are so great. I'm happy that I was invited tonight."

"You were the first one Misty mentioned," Annie says. She's also been Misty's agent for as long as she's been mine. "I know it was short notice, but this was the only weekend that worked for everyone in the coming months, so we went ahead and scheduled it. I'm glad you were able to make it."

"Like I'd miss it." I smirk and sip my cocktail. I can only have one because I can't eat in this dress, and I don't want to get hammered. I'll be starving when I get home, but it'll be worth it. "I have the interview with *Music Row* tomorrow. Do you have anything else slated for me?"

"Not yet. Do you think you'll stick around Nashville?"

"I don't know. Annie, if I want to spend more time around my family out west, what kind of a hit will my career take?"

She's quiet for a moment and then shrugs. "A lot of artists live outside of Tennessee. It might just mean more travel for you, to come here to record and for shows and parties. That sort of thing."

"But it's doable."

"Sure. But I wouldn't sell your house if I were you. You'll need a home base here."

"No, I wouldn't sell. Here's another question for you: What if I want to start doing a little promo work on my own?"

"What kind?"

"Like on social media and such. Sing new songs for the fans and see what they think, that sort of thing."

"I don't see anything wrong with it. Hell, something could blow up and we'll have labels knocking down the door again. I say do what works in all areas of your life. Sid, you're young. You're not tied to Nashville if it's not where you want to call home. You *work* here, and it'll always be here. But make your home where your heart is. Being near family is important."

"But I tour a lot," I remind us both.

"All the more reason for your permanent home to be where you're most comfortable. Spend your downtime the way *you* want to. Think of Nashville as the office."

I nod slowly, absorbing what she's saying. I like it. A lot.

"Thanks, Annie."

"You bet. I'm always a phone call away. Don't worry so much. Enjoy this beautiful life you've created for yourself."

"A beautiful life that might be falling apart," I mutter, and Annie scowls.

"Whoa. Back up. That's not the confident, take-no-prisoners Sidney I've known all these years. If this life is what you still want, you *take* it. Because no one's going to hand it to you, not even me."

I blink at her, surprised by the harsh tone in her voice, and realize that she's absolutely right.

Rather than feeling sorry for myself, I need to square my shoulders and make it happen.

"Yeah. You're right."

"Sidney, you're on in ten."

I nod at the stagehand and set the mostly full drink aside. "I'm off to take back my career."

"Atta girl."

Rick offers me a high five as we pass each other

behind the stage, and a few minutes later, I'm introduced.

"Ladies and gentlemen, my dear friend, Sidney Sterling."

I walk quickly out on the stage, holding my mic, and wave at the audience that's just exploded with hoots and hollers and applause.

It makes my heart sing.

"Hey, beautiful," I say and hug Misty over her guitar. "You having fun?"

"The time of my life." She winks at me, and we both turn to the audience.

"I just have to say a few words," I begin with a grin. "I love this woman. Misty and I go way back, singing in honky-tonks and bars here in Nashville."

"We paid our dues," Misty agrees with a laugh.

"I've toured with her, I've sung with her, and there are few people as professional and as *kind* as Misty is. I'm so incredibly proud to stand on this stage, the stage that every artist in country music holds with the highest respect, to honor you tonight. Now, we might be a couple of good girls, but even good girls…"

I hold the mic up to the audience, and they yell back at us, "Go bad!"

And with that, the band picks up with the music, and Misty and I sing our hearts out, performing for the audience.

This song is upbeat and fun, and it has the crowd dancing, up on their feet.

And when we're done, and I'm about to leave, Misty stops me.

"Hold up there, girlfriend," she says into the mic. "Before you go, I'd like to sing one of *your* songs."

I feel my eyes widen in surprise. "This night is about *you*."

"That's right, and I want to sing your 'Life in the Slow Lane'."

The crowd goes *wild*. I turn to look at the band, and they're all smiling and nodding, so I put my earpiece back in and smile.

"You got it, babe."

THE MORNING after a show like that is always slow-moving. I'm exhausted. We continued to sing for a *long* time, and Rick joined us, along with the others Misty invited to help her celebrate. Even Garth and Trisha came on stage to play with us. The cocktails poured, the pizza never stopped, and I even managed to eat a bite or two so I didn't pass out.

We had a blast.

And for the first time in a long time, I felt like I belonged. I was reminded that country music is my *home*.

I needed that.

And now, with the light of a new day, even if it is

early afternoon, I'm filled with renewed dedication and determination.

It feels like it did when I first came to Nashville, determined to make my way in the industry.

I made it happen before, and I'll do it again.

I take a couple of hours to take a nice, long shower and relax a little. I eat a salad and some bread and start making notes.

First things first, I need to make a call.

Sitting in my home office, I tap the screen of my phone and smile when I hear Stella's voice on the other end.

"Hey! We watched the show on the live stream, and, girlfriend, you *nailed* it. Also, that dress was so fucking hot on you. It made your brother totally grouchy."

"Good, that was the goal," I say with a laugh. "Hey, as much as I want to rehash everything about last night —and trust me, we will—I need a favor for now."

I'm a woman on a damn mission.

"Anything, of course. What's up?"

"Do you think Leo would be okay with you giving me his number? I need to ask him some questions, and he said that he would be totally fine talking with me, but I don't have his number."

"I just texted it to you," she says, and my phone buzzes with the incoming text. "What else?"

"I think I need to make some big changes in my life for my own happiness. I'm not giving up country music, but I'm going to do my best to live in that world on my own terms."

"Honey, this family is all about that life. We've got you."

"Awesome, thank you." My heart just keeps growing with all the love being thrown my way. "Now, I need to have a talk with Keaton, but I want to do it in person. I'm headed back to Seattle in a day or two after I get some things tied up here, but I don't want you to give him a heads-up. I'm going to surprise him."

"He's been a complete grouchy ass," Stella says, her voice dry. "*Please* make up with him, for all our sakes."

"I need to at least talk to him," I reply. "I don't know how things will turn out, but I love the grumpy ass."

"Awww," Stella says. "That's the sweetest thing *ever.*"

"It might not work out, Stella."

"Yeah, well, that's the case with every relationship. But it might work out amazingly. You're soulmates, and you'll be married for seventy-five years."

"That's a long time to be married to a cranky ass."

She laughs on the other end. "He won't be a gump because he'll be married to his soulmate."

"We'll see. Thanks, friend. I'll keep you in the loop."

"Please do. Can't wait to see you."

She clicks off, and I check one item off my list.

Only eleven more items to go.

# CHAPTER 12

## KEATON

"*D*id you watch the show the other night?"

Liam is sitting on the hood of the Jeep as I pull out the seats so I can tear off the upholstery and get it ready for new leather.

"She looked damn hot," Hudson adds from the workbench, where he's tinkering with something on the Harley he just bought. The bike is parked behind him, and it's a sweet ride. It's not brand new, by any means, but it's cool, and he'll enjoy it. He'll also take five years off his mom's life, but Aunt Meredith will be okay. He keeps talking. "That dress was smokin', and she sounded great."

They both came over on the bike to show it to me and so Hud could dick around with it here in my shop. This is where everyone comes to work on their vehicles, whether it's just an oil change or they need me to help solve something for them.

I've always loved having the family here.

Today, it's damn annoying.

Both of my cousins are quiet for a minute, and when I raise my head, I see they're both staring at me.

"What?"

"Well?" Liam demands. "Did you watch it or not?"

"Or not," I reply and get back to work.

I started to watch it, but as soon as she walked out on that stage, I knew I couldn't take it. I miss the hell out of her—everything about her, not just the sex.

Although, the sex is fucking incredible.

But I simply miss *her*. Talking with her, laughing with her. All of it.

And I've realized over the past week what a complete idiot I am. Of course, now it's too late because she's back in Nashville, back to her celebrity life, and our time together is over.

"Liv was right," Liam decides. "You *are* a grumpy ass."

I look up with a scowl. "Why the fuck were you and my sister talking about me?"

"I had lunch with her the other day at the office." He shrugs that part off. "I'm just saying, you're not usually *this* testy. Quiet, sure. Pissy? Nah, that's not you, man."

"Even if she does have a new boyfriend," Hudson mutters, and my head whips over to him.

"What the fuck?"

Hudson turns and blinks at me. "The guy she was with the other night. That Rick guy, the singer."

"You could have broken it to him a little easier than that." Liam rubs his fingers into his eye sockets.

"If he had just *watched*, it wouldn't be news to him. Sorry that she moved on so fast, man. But I guess those are the breaks when you're diddling a celebrity."

I want to punch my cousin, but it's not his fault, so I just rub my hand down my face in frustration.

"Don't kill the messenger," Liam continues. "Besides, you two weren't serious. You'll move on, too."

"Thanks for the counseling session," I reply and walk over to my bench where I have a bottle of water waiting. "What are you messing with there, Hud?"

Hudson grins. "I'm just cleaning everything up. It's running great, but I'd like you to have a quick look."

"Let's start her up."

Happy to have a distraction from talking about Sidney, we spend the next thirty minutes giving the Harley a once-over, and I declare it in excellent working order.

"What year is this?" I ask him as I reach for a rag.

"She's a 2010 Softail Deluxe," he says proudly. "Got her for under fifteen grand."

"Hell of a deal," I agree. "Who owned it before?"

"One owner," Hudson continues, rubbing his hands over the seat like he's stroking a lover. "Always garaged. I couldn't pass it up."

"It's gonna be a chick magnet," Liam says with a grin.

"Not that I need one," Hud says with a smug smile.

"Anyway, it's perfect for me, and there was room in the garage for it."

I raise an eyebrow. Hudson lives in the newest of two houses on the Cousin Compound, and I know for a fact that the house only has a two-car garage.

"How do you guys decide who gets to park in the garage?" I ask them.

"We go by age," Liam replies with a shrug. "Since Hud and I are the oldest, we get the garage."

"I moved my truck onto the street," Hudson adds. "And the bike will live in the garage."

"So, you'll keep both vehicles?" I ask him.

"Hell yes. This is Seattle. There's too much rain to only have the Harley."

"Good point."

"Sometimes, if the weather *really* sucks, we let Abby pull her convertible into the garage. I know it's weatherproof, but it's best to be sure."

"So, the living arrangements are going well? Everyone getting along okay?"

"Sure," Hudson replies. "Zoey's a neat freak and sometimes yells at Liam for leaving his socks around."

"I'll just stop wearing socks," Liam says, as if that solves everything.

"We're gonna have a compound party soon," Hudson adds. "The weather's finally good enough that we can open up the yard and the pool and spread out."

"Which is good because there are a *lot* of us."

"We're thinking about inviting the two youngest."

This comes from Liam, who frowns. "We've always said no way to the underage kids, but it's just Finn and Emma who are under twenty-one now, and we can make sure that they don't drink."

"We'll threaten them within an inch of their life." I cross my arms over my chest, thinking it over. "And if they fuck it up, they don't get invited back."

"Agreed," Liam says with a nod. "Well, we'd better get back to the house. I have to be on set in a couple of hours."

Liam's a photographer and a damn good one. Dad hired him at Williams Productions to be the film set photographer for movies they shoot nearby. And, sometimes, Liam flies out to other locations, as well.

So far, he loves it and is doing a hell of a good job.

"See you all later. Be safe on that thing."

"Yes, *Mom*."

The guys get on the Harley and take off, the engine purring like a kitten as they head down the long driveway.

So, Sid's already moved on.

That shouldn't hurt as badly as it does.

We didn't make any promises.

And she made it perfectly clear the night before she left that she was finished with me.

But fuck me, I suddenly want to beat the shit out of whoever this Rick dude is.

❧

MY EYES ARE GRITTY.

I haven't left the shop all damn day. If I go inside to rest, I'll think about Sidney, and nothing good comes from that.

I'd rather work until I can't keep my eyes open. At least I'm directing all my aggression into something productive.

I've just finished putting away my tools for the night and am ready to go inside and eat some sketchy leftover pizza and hit the shower before passing out in bed.

In that order.

Hearing footsteps behind me, I scowl and shake my head. How did I miss the roar of an engine pulling into the drive?

"Sorry, guys, the shop is closed for the day. I'm dead on my feet and headed to bed."

"Well, damn."

Every hair on my body stands on end at the sound of that perfect voice, and when I spin around and see Sidney standing in the doorway, I have to rub my eyes, sure that I'm imagining her.

But when I drop my hand, she's still there.

"Sorry it's so late," she adds. "I thought you'd be in the house, but all the lights were off, so I thought I'd try out here."

"What are you doing here?"

Yeah, my voice is way gruffer than I intended, but I'm tired.

"Well, I thought we could use a conversation."

"Look, Sidney, if you're here to bust my balls some more for being an ass before, I'm gonna save you the trouble. I already apologized, and I'm too fucking tired to spar with you right now."

She shakes her head and swallows hard, shoves her hands into the back pockets of her skin-tight jeans, and looks to the floor.

God, she's gorgeous. Sure, she was stunning in that dress on the show, from what I saw of it, but standing here, in my shop, with that tight denim and cropped sweatshirt, showing off the smooth skin of her stomach, I want her with a need that I've rarely felt before.

Hell, *never* before, except when it comes to her.

"I don't want to fight," she admits softly and steps farther into the garage. I've cut all the overhead fluorescent lights, and now there's only the glow of a single lightbulb on my trouble light, casting shadows all over the space.

She tilts her head to the side, and her high ponytail falls in a swoosh with the movement.

I want to wrap that hair around my hand, pull her head back, and bite her neck.

Instead, I turn away from her.

"Good. We agree, then. See you, Sid."

"Stop." Her voice is hard now, and I turn to see her scowling at me. "I want to have a conversation, Keaton."

"Jesus." I walk over to the utility sink in the corner

and wash my hands, then dry them on a paper towel. "Okay, if you insist, let's do that. What would you like to talk about?"

"I'm sorry, okay?"

That makes me pause.

"I've had time to give the whole situation a lot of thought, and I was wrong, too." She bites her lip. She's not wearing any makeup, which I happen to prefer on her. "I got all caught up in my excitement, and I wanted to share it with you. When you—quite firmly, by the way—made it clear that you didn't want anything to do with sharing an important moment in my life, it really hurt my feelings, and I lashed out at you. It was childish and wrong of me because you have never lied to me or made any kind of promises."

"You threw me," I admit. "We'd made it clear that we had a thing going on while you were in Seattle, and I explained to you before that I'm not willing to live any kind of public life. I thought we agreed on that."

"We did," she says, nodding. "Like I said, you never lied. I just got swept up in the thrill of it, and it was my mistake for wanting to include you in that excitement. I apologize."

My chest loosens for the first time in over a week. "Thank you for that."

Sidney nods, pulls her hands out of her pants, and takes a few steps toward me.

"I hear you've moved on."

That makes her stop cold and frown at me. "What?"

187

"With the country star."

She shakes her head slowly, scowling as if she doesn't know what I'm talking about, and then her face clears, and she shakes her head.

"Oh, no. Rick and I are friends. We were both going to the event and decided to go together, that's all."

Now the knots in my stomach loosen.

"So, no man in Nashville waiting for you?"

"No." She takes a few steps toward me. "Keaton, I don't know how you've missed it, but *you're* the one I'm interested in."

"How did I *miss* it?" I demand with a laugh. "Oh, I don't know….. You threw me out of the condo when I tried to apologize. You made it clear that we were done."

"No, I didn't. I made it clear that I was *pissed*. Those are two very different things."

"Not from where I'm standing."

She blows out a breath, curses under her breath, and kicks at something on the floor.

"Have I fucked this up beyond repair?" she finally asks, turning to me with so much emotion rolling through her gorgeous blue eyes, it's almost my undoing. "I mean, I know I messed up, but is it too bad to fix it?"

"No," I finally admit. "And if I'm being brutally honest, we *both* did some fucking up here. I could have communicated better, and I should have tried harder. But I think we need to establish what it is that we're fixing here, Sidney. Is it still friends with benefits whenever you're in Seattle?"

She frowns, and her hands ball into fists and then relax again, as if she wants to reach out for me, so I put us both out of our misery and reach out to take her hand in mine.

Sidney sighs in relief and walks right into my arms, buries her face in my chest, and holds on tight.

"I really missed you," she admits, her voice muffled against my shirt. "Even though you smell bad."

My lips twitch at that, and I bury them in her hair. "I work with grease."

"Yeah." She pulls back and keeps my hand in hers. "Are you hungry?"

That's code for *feed me.*

"I was just closing up the shop. Let's go inside and get some pizza. I'll take a quick shower, and we can continue this talk."

"Thank God you didn't kick me out of here."

"I'm a sucker for you," I reply truthfully as I lock up the shop and take her hand once more to walk to the house. "There's no car in the driveway."

"I know." She shrugs. "I had Gray drop me off."

"What if I *had* kicked you out?"

"He would have come to get me. He might have beat you up while he was at it, though."

I chuckle as we walk into my house. I know we have a lot to talk about, and I can't wait to get my hands on her properly, but first things first.

"I'm gonna hop in the shower so I don't stink anymore," I tell her. "There's leftover pizza in the fridge."

She eyes me warily. "How long has it been in there?"

"I don't know...a few days."

"Go." She waves me off, reaching for her phone. "Take a shower. I'll cover dinner."

I'm no longer as tired as I was fifteen minutes ago as I walk into the bathroom and start the shower. While it heats up, I quickly shave and brush my teeth, then hop into the hot water.

I don't hurry. There's no need to. Sidney will be here all night, and I've already waited a week to see her.

So, I take my time in the shower, already feeling so much better but unwilling to let myself hope for too much because, at the end of the day, this could all fall apart again.

When I'm clean and dressed, I walk out to the living room and find Sid curled up at the end of my couch, one of the beers from my fridge in her hand.

"I got one out for you," she says, gesturing to the other bottle on the coffee table. "Pizza will be here in about fifteen minutes."

"Thanks." I want to sit next to her and pull her into my lap, but instead, I grab the beer and sit in the chair across from her. "Where are you staying?"

"At the condo." She sips the beer. "I never let it go. I like it there. So, let's talk this out, okay? Because I don't like misunderstandings."

"Okay. My previous question stands. Are we still going to do the hookup thing when you're in Seattle?"

"No." She blows out a breath and sets her beer aside, rubbing her hands over her face. "I mean, yes, we'll be hooking up, but I don't think that's all I want from you anymore, Keaton. I caught feelings somewhere along the line, and I can't turn them off."

"I can't change the way I feel about your celebrity status," I say quietly as she watches me with those big blue eyes. "I'm sorry, but I just *can't*. And I would never ask you to choose."

"I wouldn't choose," she replies flatly. "Because I wouldn't ever be with someone who would ask me to. But, I think we can make this work. I refuse to believe that I can't have both. I still have some things to work out, but I'd like to try."

"I think, as long as I stay out of camera range, and you understand that I'll always hang back when it comes to the spotlight, we can move forward."

Finally, hope sets up residence in her eyes.

"Did you catch feelings, too?"

I grin and pat my leg, inviting her to sit on my lap.

She scurries over, sits, and wraps her arms around my neck.

"It's okay," she whispers in my ear. "You can admit if you caught the feelings. I won't tell your secret."

I laugh now and, with my finger under her chin, tip her face up so I can kiss the hell out of her.

God, I missed the taste of her. The feel of her in my arms.

The past week was absolute torture.

"I caught *all* of the feelings, sweetheart. It was never one-sided."

She moans and shifts to straddle me, cups my face, and continues to kiss me as my hands roam under her short sweatshirt, over her bare skin.

"You're not wearing a bra."

She grins as she stares down at me. "It's just easier that way."

We're a tangle of lips and hands, moans and sighs, until we eventually make it onto the floor, struggling out of clothes.

"Bedroom." I stand and lift her, toss her over my shoulder, and smack her little ass.

"I don't think I've ever had makeup sex before," she announces with a loud giggle and then shrieks when I toss her onto the mattress. "I think I like it."

"Oh, you're gonna love it." Reaching for a condom, I urge Sidney onto her stomach, but when she pushes up on her knees, I hold her down, pressing on the small of her back. "I didn't say you could do that."

"Oh, God, I love it when you're bossy."

I straddle her hips, and with my thumbs, gently spread her open. She glistens with need, and I easily push right inside of her, making us both groan.

"Missed you," she whispers and grips the pillow with fisted hands. "God, I missed you."

I can't hold myself back from pushing harder and harder, going faster. I'm a man possessed, *obsessed.*

And when she cries out with her orgasm, I rock against her and then pull out, roll her over, and push right back in.

"Oh, God."

"Say my name," I demand. "Open those gorgeous eyes and say my fucking name."

I circle her throat with my hand but don't squeeze.

"Keaton," she groans. "Oh, fuck, I'm gonna come again."

I lean down to press my lips to her ear as she begins to come apart, even harder than the last time.

"Mine," I growl into her ear. "This, all of this, is mine."

"Holy shit."

"Say it."

She licks her lips and then whispers, "Yours. Fucking yours."

"That's right." I fall over the edge into paradise with her, feeling all the pieces of my life fit back together. "That's fucking right."

"I think I hear the pizza guy pulling in," she says, still catching her breath. "I'm extra hungry now."

"Makeup sex *and* makeup pizza? I like the sound of that. You stay there. I'll take care of it."

"I get pizza in bed?" The hopeful look on her gorgeous face makes me laugh. "Best day ever."

# CHAPTER 13

## SIDNEY

"Why am I so nervous? I already met the man. Played with him and everything."

"Don't be nervous," Keaton advises with a soft smile and wraps his arms around me from behind, watching me in the mirror. "It's just coffee and conversation. My uncle Leo isn't a scary guy. If you want scary, that would be Caleb, Matt—hell, even Uncle Dom has his intense moments. Leo's harmless."

"Have I met your uncle Dom?"

He grins and kisses my cheek. In the few days that I've been back, we've settled into this cozy routine of spending most of our free time together, making meals, watching TV, and having sex.

This morning, we worked out together. To my surprise, Keaton has a small workout area in one of the bedrooms in the back of the house that someone once used as an office. He threw a weight rack and some dumbbells in there, and it's actually a really great space.

Of course, we ended up naked on the mat, but I just count that as part of the exercise.

"Yes," he says, bringing me out of my sensual memory. "You met Dom at Liv's wedding. He's the tall Italian guy."

"Oh, yeah, the one with the accent?"

"That's him."

"Why does he have an accent? No one else does."

"He was raised in Italy."

I turn in his arms and frown up at him. "How did that happen?"

"Well, super long story short, no one knew he existed until shortly after Liv was born. At one point, my grandma and grandpa split for a very short time. He had an affair during that split, and Dominic was the result of that. But the mom never told Grandpa about it, and after she died, Dom came looking for his father."

"Wow, you have the most interesting family."

"Tell me about it." He kisses my forehead and backs away. "You ready to go?"

"I think so." I check myself in the mirror one last time. I didn't do much with my hair, but I did put on a little makeup. It's rainy and chilly outside today, so I'm in jeans and a T-shirt, layered with a cute sweatshirt from my tour.

"Let's go." Keaton leads me out to his Bronco, and he drives me into the heart of the city. Leo invited me to coffee at Nic's bakery, which I've been to a few times and always indulge in the strawberry shortcake cupcakes.

They're heaven.

"I'm headed to Will's to tweak his new Mustang," Keaton says as he pulls up to the curb. "He says it sounds funny."

"You literally just handed the keys to him."

"It's an older car. They're temperamental. It's fine. Just let me know when you want me to come get you."

"My condo isn't far," I reply, shaking my head. "I'll walk home."

"It's raining."

"I know I'm sweet, but I won't melt. I promise. I'll call you later, okay?"

"Okay, have fun. If you change your mind, you know how to reach me."

I grin and lean over to kiss him. "Thanks. See you later."

I hop out of the Bronco and walk inside, the sweet smell of sugar and coffee welcoming me like a big hug.

I have one hell of a sweet tooth.

Leo's standing at the counter, chatting with Nic, and when the bell over the door dings, they both turn to see who it is, smiling when they see me.

"There she is," Leo says. "My lovely coffee date."

"Hi, Sidney," Nic says with a soft smile. "What can I get for you?"

"I'd love a coffee with cream and one of those addictive strawberry shortcake cupcakes."

"You got it. Go ahead and grab a seat, you two. I'll bring it out to you."

Leo nods and gestures for me to choose a table. I love the décor in here. The floor is black-and-white tile, with little round tables and chairs with shiny red seats, just like an old-timey café.

I choose a seat by the window, and Leo sits across from me.

"I caught your performance at the Opry," he says with a grin. "You killed it."

"It was a lot of fun. Have you played the Opry?"

"No, I'm not country enough for them, and I completely understand."

I nod and glance out the window to the building across the street. "Is that a studio?"

"It is. I'm recording there later today, in fact. I haven't recorded an album in LA in *years*. We do everything either across the street there or in my home studio. Technology is a beautiful thing."

"I love that," I admit, giving the building another look.

"We can walk over there when we're done here, and I can give you a tour."

"If it's not an imposition, that would be great."

"Not at all," he assures me. "Are you kidding? We always love bringing in established artists to play around. Now, as happy as I am to sit here and shoot the shit, I assume you asked to meet for a reason."

Before I can reply, Nic walks over, holding a tray full of our orders. She sets our coffees down as well as a cupcake for each of us.

Leo chose chocolate.

"Enjoy, you two," Nic says and walks away.

I glance down to where Leo wraps his hands around his mug of coffee. He has tattoos down his hands and fingers.

Leo has tattoos *everywhere*, and they're damn sexy.

But that's not why I'm here.

"You mentioned before, when we were at your house, that I could reach out if I needed advice."

He nods and lifts his mug to his lips.

"I guess I need a *lot* of advice right now." I shake my head and sip my own coffee.

"Start at the beginning, and we'll work our way through it."

He's so...*calm*. So easy to talk to.

"Okay, first of all, I lost my contract with the label." Leo's eyes narrow, and I fill him in on the dismal album and tour sales. "So, when I came off the tour, I was informed that they didn't want to renew for a new album."

"Why do you think it failed?"

My eyes widen at that word. *Failed.*

"Listen, I'm blunt. This is business. Get your feelings out of it for a minute, and think about it as a businesswoman, because that's exactly what you are. Why do you think the album failed?"

I sigh and do as he says. I set my personal feelings aside and think it over. "The music was different from anything I'd done before. I was trying to show the audience that I'd grown up, that I'd evolved as an artist. Maybe they want me to sing the same kind of songs over and over again."

"Don't guess. Just tell me what you know."

I take another sip of coffee. "Okay. The tone of the album wasn't as *country* as I've done before. It had more of a pop sound to it, and the tour incorporated more dancing, more lights, and more pyrotechnics than me with my band."

Leo doesn't say anything; he simply leans back in his chair, listening.

"I veered too far off from what my fans love about my music and my performances. I can have the pyro and lights, but I need to make sure there's a balance."

"There you go. There's nothing wrong with trying new things, but you do that one song at a time, not an entire album. Now you have to earn back the trust of your fans."

I bite my lip, drumming my fingernails on the table. "I need new music."

"Agreed."

"Someone recently told me that I should get on social media, have a presence there, with some new songs."

"I think that works well for the artists your age."

"You don't have social media?"

Leo grins and peels the paper off his cupcake. "We have a social media manager. She's a gem. Hell no, I don't want to do that shit. Our girl takes video of us, interviews us, records us in the studio or on stage, and shares it on the platforms. But I think, to start, you need to have a personal presence."

"I do, too. I'd like to play the song that we wrote. I've done some tweaking and made it sound a little more country."

"I can't wait to hear it," he says with a grin, and I can tell by the excitement in his eyes that he means it.

"Can I say that I cowrote it with you?"

"Of course. You did. And you're welcome to write with me anytime. That was damn fun."

I smile, lighting up from the inside. "It really was fun. I'd love to write with you or collaborate with you. I don't want to overstep, but maybe we could do a duet sometime."

"I'm in," he replies immediately. "What did you call the song?"

"'Little Miss.'" I grin over at him. "It's repeated in the chorus a lot, and I think it works with my brand."

"I like it." He nods. "Are you keeping it a ballad?"

"Yeah, a lot of guitar and piano. Very moody."

"*Love* moody," he says. "I can't wait to hear it. If you want to record it, come over to my place next week, and we'll get it down for you."

I blink at him, shocked. "Really?"

"Why not? Do you really need more *time off*?" He tilts his head and gives me the look that says, *I already know how you'll respond to this.*

"No. I don't. I'm ready to sing and record. I'm not ready to tour, but yes, on the music."

"Then let's make some music. You're not under contract. You can do whatever the fuck you want."

"I NEED to grab that package that was delivered the other day," I say to my brother when he opens the door to his condo. "And hi, by the way."

"Hey, come on in. The box is right here. It's fucking heavy. What did you order?"

"Everyone told me that I need a ring light to make good videos for social media, so I ordered one of those. And while I was shopping, I found some cool note-books, another hoodie I didn't need, and a bag of Twizzlers."

He blinks at me. "That's a wide variety of shit."

"Amazon." I shrug. "Where's Stella?"

"She's out at the vineyard with her mom, Liv, and

Natalie. She's decided she wants to get married out there."

"I don't blame her. Liv's wedding was *gorgeous*. It's the perfect place for it. Are you still thinking about late summer?"

"Next month," he replies, shaking his head.

"*Next month*?" I scowl and reach out to smack his arm. "Jesus, were you going to tell any of us?"

"She just decided *yesterday*."

"Next month is in two weeks."

"Three weeks until the wedding. She's ready. Hell, I'm *more* than ready. It's time."

"I'm so happy for you. I love Stella. I love the entire family. They're awesome, Gray."

"I know. They're big and loud and kind of crazy sometimes, but there's never a dull moment, and I've never met a family like them."

"How heavy is this box?" I squat next to it and lift it, only struggling a little. "Shit, I ordered too much."

"Need me to carry it down for you?"

"Nah, I got it. Just get the door for me."

Gray follows me down the hallway to get the elevator for me, too, and waves as the doors close.

"Three weeks," I mutter. "What will I wear? I need a wine night with Stella."

The doors open on my floor, and I step out and walk down the hall to my rental.

I have to set the box down to unlock the door, but I manage to muscle it inside. I haven't been here in a couple of days because I've been staying with Keaton.

Which has been awesome, but I like having my own place, too. I've always been independent.

I turn up the heat a little to take the chill off and walk into the bedroom to change into yoga pants and a cropped sweatshirt.

If I'm going to perform live on an app, I need to look comfortable but still a little trendy, according to Keaton's cousins.

I'm going to take their word for it.

I put on a little more makeup and then get to work, opening the big box with the treasures inside.

"Oh, I forgot I bought these." I set the bag of pens I forgot all about aside and pull out the biggest bag of Twizzlers I've ever seen. "I guess I should read the description of things when I'm shopping online."

The ring light is in its own box at the bottom.

And it takes me thirty minutes to figure out how to put it together.

"I hate this kind of crap," I mutter and blow my hair out of my face. "I'm sweating, for Christ's sake."

I have to step back and prop my hands on my hips and catch my breath.

Who knew this would be so strenuous? I have a new respect for influencers. I'll have to tell Sophie that the next time I see her.

Finally, after blinding myself when I turn on the light, I have everything set up the way I want it and prop my phone in the little holder thingy in the middle of the light.

"I need sunglasses," I mutter as I turn and reach for my guitar.

When I'm all situated, I bring up the app that Sophie helped me download and get signed up for and see that I already have over a quarter-million followers.

Holy shit.

How did that happen?

I press the *Live* button, and while the app does its thing, I do mine, making sure my guitar is tuned just right. I glance at the phone and see that people are already commenting.

"Do I really have ten thousand people here?" I ask out loud, surprised. "Wow! Hi, everyone! Hey. This is my very first time here on the app, and I thought I'd come hang out with you all for a little while. Whoa, the comments are going really fast. Sorry, guys, I won't be able to keep up with that. I'll try to get better, okay?"

I smile, a little overwhelmed by the number of people already here, and then take a quick drink of water.

"I thought I'd sing a little song for y'all tonight. I hope that's okay."

Hearts explode on the screen, so I assume they're okay with the idea.

"This song is new. *Brand* new. I wrote it a few weeks ago with a guy I'm sure you all know, Leo Nash. He was kind enough to let me sit in on a writing session with him and our friend, Brax Adler. Now, I know those two guys are rock stars, and I'm a country singer, but I think you're going to be pleasantly surprised by what we came up with."

More hearts fill the screen, and that boosts my confidence.

"The song is called 'Little Miss'. And I'm not going to tell you anything else about it because I want you to *hear* it. So, here we go."

I check the screen once more and see that there are now twenty-five thousand people here with me, and I blow out a breath to settle my nerves.

Why is this harder than singing in front of an arena full of people?

I begin to strum the strings and settle into the song. Like I told Leo, it's so moody, just in the middle of my register, so I'm able to really sink in and just *live* in the song.

By the time I hit the chorus, I'm fully absorbed, loving every word, every note.

And when I've finished, I glance up at the screen and see it explode with red hearts. They go on for what seems like an hour, and I take that to mean that they're applauding.

"Thanks, everyone." I smile at the phone. "Really, I'm so glad y'all like that song. It's pretty special to me. Now, while I'm here, go ahead and shout out a few requests, and I'll play a couple. What would you like to hear?"

I lean in to read some of the comments.

*Best voice in country music!*

*You sound like an angel!*

*Marry me.*

*You need to wear more clothes.*

*Wow, okay. We give life advice on here. Good to know.*

Finally, requests start popping up, but the one that always blows the others away is "Life in the Slow Lane".

"It always makes me so happy that y'all love that song," I say as I return to my guitar. "I wrote it a long time ago, but I feel like it continues to resonate with me. I'm glad it does you, too. Okay, let's do this."

As I begin to play the guitar, my front door opens, and Keaton walks in. His eyes narrow when he sees my setup, and understanding immediately what I'm doing, he quietly closes the door and moves soundlessly to the piano.

"You're going to hear the piano in the background," I inform my listeners. "I have a friend here who wants to stay off camera. But this is going to get *good*."

I grin, and as Keaton adds the piano, I start to sing, and just as I did before, I let the song wash over me until I'm unaware of everything else.

It's just me and the music.

When the last notes fade away, I glance back at Keaton, who's watching me with green eyes full of something I can't quite put my finger on.

And I don't have time to explore it right now, with so many people watching.

"This has been fun," I say with a big smile. "It's something I'll definitely do again. Thanks for hanging out with me tonight. Take care of yourselves out there, okay? Love you, guys."

I reach out and stop the video, and then I let out a gusty breath and turn to Keaton.

"That went well."

"You're fucking incredible."

# CHAPTER 14

## KEATON

"*I*'ve outgrown streaking."

Hudson and I share a look and then bust up laughing.

"Why? Because you're an old man of twenty-six now?" Hudson asks.

"Well, yeah," Liam admits. "And I have to say, it makes me a little sad. I've moved on to a new phase in my life."

"And what phase is that?" Drew wants to know. He's been standing behind Liam, listening.

"Adulthood."

We all snicker again.

"You'll be in that phase until the day you die." I pat Liam on the shoulder. "However, I see that you're still wearing those loud-ass Hawaiian shirts."

"No one said that I can't wear my shirts." He's defensive as he looks down at the blue-and-green monstrosity he's wearing. "I like them. They're fun. And they're comfortable. So leave my shirts alone."

Stella happens to be walking by and raises an eyebrow. "Who's giving my Liam a hard time? I'll punch them out."

"All of these assholes," Liam says, pointing to us. "Kick all their asses."

She could. Stella's a badass.

"Don't make me break all your noses," she says with a glare and then moves on.

"I'm Stella's favorite," Liam says with a proud grin. "Anyway, what's up with all of you?"

"I'm moving out," Drew announces and raises his beer in cheers. "I love living in the compound, but I think I'm taking that job with the pro team, and I'd like a place closer to work. It was fun while it lasted, and I'm grateful for the opportunity that our parents give us to live here, but it's time to give up my room to someone else."

"So, you've officially been offered the position?" I ask him.

"Yeah. Uncle Will accepted his offer—one that I'm sure he would have been *really* stupid to refuse—last week, and then he immediately turned around and offered me the defensive line coaching position. I can't turn it down. Hell, I don't *want* to turn it down."

"Congratulations, man. Has someone already called dibs on your room at the compound?" I ask him.

"I don't think so." Drew shrugs. "Only Finn and

Emma are left at home, and I doubt their parents will let them move anywhere until they graduate."

"Makes sense," Liam says. "Okay, who's gonna sing karaoke with me?"

"Dude, you're not drunk enough for that."

"Sure, I am." He winks and sets off in search of a partner in crime.

"I have an announcement," Stella yells out, clapping her hands. "Shut up and listen to me, damn it."

"You're such an attention whore," someone calls out, but Stella only laughs and strikes a pose.

"I take that as a compliment. Anyway, Gray and I are getting married in two weeks. Invitations are in the mail, but I'm also spreading the word myself because we know it's short notice. Whatever you have on the calendar, clear it. None of you are missing my wedding."

"Why so fast?" Haley calls out. "Are you knocked up?"

A gasp rolls through the crowd of cousins, but Stella only laughs.

"I wish it was that interesting. No, we've just been waiting for a long time for the *perfect* time, and that's not going to happen. So, I picked a day, and we're doing it. It'll be at the vineyard, and we mostly invited super close friends and all of the family."

"So, it'll be a huge wedding," Olivia adds, making us all laugh.

"Hey, we love a lot of people." Stella shrugs, then

blows us all a kiss. "I love you guys so much. It would kill me if you weren't there, so plan on it, okay?"

"Wouldn't miss it," I reply and look around the backyard for my date.

Sidney is standing next to Gray, her eyes glassy with happy tears, and I decide that I've had enough chitchat with these jerks and set off to claim her.

"Don't cry," I say as I wrap my arm around her and kiss her temple.

"I'm just so happy for them," she says, wiping under her eyes. "They're so *happy*."

"I hope so. They're getting hitched."

She laughs and then leans her head on my shoulder. "There are always so many people at your family parties. I don't know why it surprises me every time."

"And the parents aren't even here this time."

My gaze skims the crowd, looking for our two underage kids, and I see Finn and Emma, sitting side by side at the edge of the pool, their feet in the water, drinking cans of soda.

"They better not have laced those sodas with vodka."

"How old are those two?" Sidney asks, following my gaze.

"They're both graduating high school in a few weeks. But they're eighteen and the only two left underage. So, we decided to include them, with strict rules."

"Looks to me like they're having fun, laughing and

talking, and they probably appreciate being included with the 'big kids'."

"Yeah, they seem fine."

"Sidney!"

We glance over as Abby and Zoey hurry our way.

"Your video!" Zoey's bouncing up and down. "Ohmygosh, this is fucking incredible."

"What?" Sidney demands. "What happened?"

"You have three *million* views," Abby informs Sidney. "On just that one video of you singing 'Little Miss'."

"Is that a lot?" Sidney asks.

The two women look at each other, then back to Sidney. "Yes! It's viral. This is a great thing."

"You're getting more views on the other couple of videos you made, too," Zoey adds. "I'm *so* proud of you."

"How do you two know this?" I ask them, and they just roll their eyes at me.

"We follow her," Zoey says slowly, as if I'm completely clueless.

Which, I am.

"We're paying attention because she's part of the family now," Abby puts in. "And it's just so awesome to watch. I love that you wrote the song with Uncle Leo. Who knew that he could write a country song?"

"It wasn't country when we first wrote it," Sidney replies. "He gave me permission to take it and tweak it for my audience. I'm *so* glad that people are loving it."

"They do," Zoey says. "And what's not to love? They'd be stupid if they didn't love it."

"We just had to let you know, in case you weren't paying attention," Abby says. "We follow you, Sophie, our cousin Amelia, Ike...you know, everyone in the family."

"Well, thanks," Sid says. "Thanks a lot. And if you have any suggestions for things I should do for the socials, please tell me. I don't know how to do this stuff."

"Give us your number, and we can text you ideas," Abby suggests.

The three of them exchange numbers, and then the other two are off to find another drink.

"That's so sweet," Sidney says.

"Yeah, they don't suck. Hey, where's Maya?"

Sid grins and looks around with me. Maya was able to come over to Seattle for the weekend to see how her mom handles less constant care. The family felt comfortable with it, given how well Jeanie's been doing, and Maya deserved a break.

"I don't know," Sidney says with a frown. "I don't see her."

"Maybe she's inside, getting some food."

"Let's go see." Sid grabs my hand and leads me through the yard to the back door of the original Alki house that's been in the family forever. My mom bought it when she was younger than I am now.

"Here are some more chips," I hear Maya say as she

opens a bag and begins to fill a bowl. "I think there are more burgers on the grill outside. Go ask Drew. It's his turn on grill duty."

I snicker, but Sidney frowns.

"Uh, Maya?"

The beautiful woman's head comes up at the sound of my voice.

"Yeah? What do you need?"

"Nothing. Honey, you're a *guest* here, not a waitress."

She cringes, then shrugs. "Sorry. I can't sit still. I have to *do* stuff, and when I came in here and saw that the platters needed to be refilled, I just did it. It's no big deal. Unless you'd rather I didn't—"

"As long as you're having fun," Sidney interrupts. "That's the whole point of you being here this weekend."

"Oh, I am. It's really nice to get away for a little while, you know? And everyone is so nice. I'm about done here anyway."

"How do you remember everyone's names?" Sidney asks her sister quietly. "Because I wish they all wore nametags."

Maya laughs and waves Sidney off. "I've always been good with names."

"I need a spreadsheet," Sid says with a scowl, making me laugh.

"I'll make you one," I reply and kiss her hair.

"Come sing karaoke with me," Liam says, taking the

bag of chips out of Maya's hands and tossing it aside. "I need a duet partner."

Maya's wide eyes find her sister's. "Uh, I'm not really the singer in the family."

"Don't care," Liam says as he drags her away, and now Sidney's laughing.

"Don't look now, but I think your cousin is flirting with my sister."

I shake my head, watching them in the corner of the living room, mics in hand. "He won't do anything she doesn't want him to."

"She needs to be pulled, literally, out of her comfort zone now and then. I'm not surprised that she slipped right into the role of hostess. She's a mother hen."

"She's actually really adorable."

Sidney's face whips up to look at me.

"Don't worry, I only have eyes for you, babe. I'm just saying your sister is sweet, and I'm glad she was able to come over here for a few days."

"Me, too. We're having a little bridal shower for Stella tomorrow, and Mom's going to join us via video call."

"What?" I frown down at her. "Why video?"

"It's a decent drive from their house to Seattle, and I think it's best if she only does it once, so she'll come for the wedding."

"That's absolutely ridiculous." I shake my head and pull out my phone.

"What do you mean? Keaton, what are you doing?"

"She shouldn't miss the shower tomorrow. You said she's been feeling well and in good health?"

"Well, sure, but—"

I hold up a finger to shut her up, and her eyes turn into sapphire slits.

It makes me grin.

"Hey, are you guys okay?" Dad asks when he answers the phone.

"Yeah, we're having a good time. Everything's under control here. I need a favor."

"Name it."

I smile down at the woman I've completely fallen in love with when I wasn't looking and say, "Would you be willing to use your plane to get Sidney's mom from Idaho and bring her here for Stella's shower tomorrow and then take her home when she's ready?"

"Of course." There's no hesitation in my dad's voice. No hint of irritation.

Sidney's shaking her head, but I just continue to smile.

"Thanks, Dad. They don't want her to do the drive twice in the same month, but she's pretty healthy and should be okay with the short flight."

"I'll start making arrangements right now. I have the Sterlings' number. I'll call and get everything organized on their end, too. Good idea, Keaton. I'll make sure they have the jet for the wedding, as well."

"Thank you. Appreciate it."

"Think nothing of it. Talk soon."

He hangs up, and I push my phone back into my pocket. Sidney has tears running down her cheeks, and she launches herself into my arms and kisses me like her life depends on it.

The whole party erupts in applause and cheers, and I hear Stella yell, "Get a room!"

"Thank you," Sidney says against my lips, staring into my eyes. "Thank you *so much.* You didn't have to do that."

"Your mom shouldn't miss out."

She hugs me close and buries her face in my neck. "I can't believe I'm saying this right here, right now, but I love you, Keaton. For a million reasons, and your kindness is right at the top."

Consumed with emotion, I turn and walk around the side of the house where there's a little more privacy.

"Hey," I begin, but she shakes her head and swallows hard.

"I mean it. I've fallen so deeply in love with you, and I don't know when exactly it happened, but it did, and I just had to tell you, even if it was in front of your whole family."

"They couldn't hear you." I brush my fingers down her cheek, wiping away her tears. "I love you, too, sweetheart."

"Now I've turned into one of those mushy people that I make fun of."

"It's okay." I kiss her softly. "I'll make fun of you later."

"Dude!" Liam points at Gray, a beer in his hand and a huge grin on his face. "You're getting married *tomorrow!*"

"That's not a lie," Gray says with a laugh.

All of us guys, including Gray's dad, are at my uncle Will's for the bachelor party. Gray didn't want anything wild and crazy—no strippers, nothing…hardcore.

So, Will invited us all to come here for food—with Will, there's always food—pool, ping-pong, and to watch sports on Will's multiple screens, pretty much all the testosterone-filled things that a guy could want.

Gray's been eating it up.

Ike invited a couple of the guys from the team, and Gray included some of his attorney friends, as well.

It's the place to be tonight in Seattle. The press would have a fucking field day.

Of course, all the women are at the Four Seasons in the city tonight for pampering, girl-style.

Sidney was beside herself with excitement at the idea of getting a massage.

Little does she know, she's getting much more than that.

My phone pings with a message, and I glance down and grin.

*Sidney: YOU SENT ME FLOWERS!*

*Me: One for every time I'll think of you tonight.*

The bubble jumps on my screen as she replies.

*Sidney: There are twelve roses. You're only going to think of me twelve times?*

*Me: You're greedy.*

*Sidney: You bet your fine ass. Thanks, babe. xo*

I pop my phone back into my pocket and look up to find my dad smiling at me.

"What?"

"You're completely smitten with that girl."

"Only old people use the word *smitten*."

His smile doesn't waver.

"I'm just doing some nice things for her. She deserves them."

And I've watched my dad shower my mom with little gifts and thoughtful things my whole life. He swears that it's the way to a woman's heart.

So far, it's working.

Sidney especially seems to love having me bring her coffee in bed. I've had a lot of grateful sex, thanks to that.

"Keep that up," he advises with a wink. "I'm happy for you."

Without asking me any questions, he walks away to join Isaac and Matt at the ping-pong table, where Matt is kicking Isaac's ass, and a whole group of guys is standing around, cheering them on.

I walk into the house to see what there is to eat when my phone pings again.

*Sidney: Now you sent enough mini cherry cobblers for all of us!*

I grin and simply dial her number.

"Hi, sweetheart," I say when she picks up.

"You're spoiling me! You know that cherry cobbler is my favorite."

"I know. It's a special night. You should enjoy it. And everyone loves cobbler."

There's some murmuring in the background and then Sidney giggles.

"My mom just said that you're a keeper. I'm so glad that she's here, Keaton. Thank your dad for me, okay?"

"I will. And she's totally right. Listen to your mom. I won't keep you on the line. Go enjoy your time with the girls."

"I'm gonna eat this cobbler and then go sit in the steam room with Stella and Sophie. They want to drill me about our relationship."

"Of course, they do. Have fun, babe."

"Okay, we will. Love you, bye."

She's gone before I can tell her I love her, too. Every time she says it to me, it's like a punch to the gut, but in a good way.

I can't explain it.

"Was that my daughter's voice I heard?"

I turn and find Sidney's father smiling at me from the other side of the kitchen island. He's a tall man, with thinning dark hair and a kind smile. David's been nothing but kind to me in the few times I've met him.

"Yes, it was Sidney. I owe you an apology, Dr. Sterling."

His eyebrows climb in surprise. "Why is that?"

"Because I haven't come to see you in person to tell you that I've been seeing your daughter and that I've fallen in love with her."

He nods slowly, leaning on the counter. "Well, better late than never, I suppose. It may sound old-fashioned, but what are your intentions where Sidney is concerned?"

I blow out a breath and push my hand through my hair.

"I can't imagine my life without her in it. I know that we have very different lifestyles, but I hope that, with time, we can figure things out. One day, I'd like to marry her."

"Are you asking my permission for that?"

"Yes, sir, I guess I am."

He's quiet for a minute as he stares down at the countertop. "You know, I always knew that Sidney was going to make a splash in the world. Shake it up a bit. And I also knew that the man who ended up loving her was going to have his hands full with her. She's so easy to love, but she's not *easy*, if that makes sense."

"Yeah." I nod and can't help but chuckle. "That's exactly how I'd describe her, too."

"If and when you decide to propose to my girl, you have my blessing. On one condition."

"Okay…"

He narrows his eyes at me. "You have to be prepared to love *everything* about her, all the way. Sidney flourishes under the spotlight. She always has. It's going to be a part of your life whether you like it or not. You have to know that if you don't embrace and love and support every bit of her, including the pieces that aren't easy, it won't work for you two. Because asking her to choose would just be cruel."

Every word is a stab right into my heart.

Because he's absolutely right.

I love and *crave* this downtime with her, when Nashville isn't knocking on her door and she can just be Sidney, my girlfriend.

The rest of it still makes me damn nervous.

"Thanks for that," I reply and reach out to shake the other man's hand. "It makes a lot of sense and gives me a lot to think about."

"I'm always a phone call away if you need to talk."

He turns to return to the party, and I stay behind, my mind whirling.

I have a lot to think about.

## CHAPTER 15

### SIDNEY

"*H*ow many of the cousins are hung over today?" I ask Keaton as I fasten my diamond stud earring in place and watch this man that I love tie his tie in the mirror behind me.

"Too many," he says. "We had a good time at Uncle Will's. Gray didn't get drunk, though. He's too smart for that. Did you girls get hammered?"

"No." I snort and turn to pull my dress off the hanger and step into it. It's a pink strapless number that shows off my legs, per usual. "We *relaxed.* We ate delicious food and had body treatments, and we talked. A *lot* of talking. I mean, sure, there was some champagne, but we didn't go crazy with it. We had too much food to soak it all up."

When Keaton unknots his tie for the third time in frustration, I bat his hands out of the way and get to work on it myself.

223

"We have to be there in an hour," he reminds me, watching my face as I focus on his tie. "Are you about ready to go?"

"I just have to grab my bag," I assure him as I cinch up the tie and smooth it down with my fingers. "There. You look hot in a suit, Mr. Williams."

"I hate wearing these things," he admits with a scowl and shakes his head, turning back to the mirror to make sure his hair is just so. "But I'll do it for Stella."

"You guys are so much more than cousins. All of you. It's like there are a million siblings in your family."

"Yeah, we're tight. Always have been."

I smooth on some lipstick, reach for my small clutch, and grin at my hot-as-hell date. "Let's go. I want to see Gray before this shindig gets started."

Keaton came to my condo this morning, his suit and everything he needed in a bag, and we got ready together.

Now we're heading down to the parking garage, where his Bronco is parked.

It's Saturday, but it's early enough in the day that traffic through Seattle isn't horrible. And soon, we're headed out of town, toward the vineyard.

"How long has your uncle owned this place?"

"Long time," Keaton says. "I don't know when he bought it, but it's been in the family since before I was born. It's gone through some changes, of course. Uncle Dom has added grapes, taken some out, and they added a whole new building onto the bed-and-breakfast. It's kind of a big deal."

"I love it out there." I sit back, getting cozy in the seat. For being an older vehicle, Keaton sure made the Bronco comfy when he restored it. "I think it's the perfect spot for a wedding."

He's quiet, and I can't help but laugh and reach over to push my fingers into the back of his hair.

"Don't worry, I'm not fishing for a proposal or anything. Just saying it's so beautiful at the vineyard. It's perfect for weddings. And it's private, so it really cuts down on the press."

"That's the best part." He takes my hand and kisses my palm. "I'll always welcome a no-press day."

"I know. And I'm sure the rest of the family agrees."

"It's a big factor in why so many big events for the family are held out there. It's the largest estate in the family, and Uncle Dom can control the press. From what I hear, we've been having weddings and big parties out at the vineyard since before I was born. I think Uncle Will and Aunt Meg were the first to have a wedding there."

"But not Brax and Josie?"

He shakes his head and takes the exit off the freeway. "Nah, they eloped. Josie didn't want anything big and splashy, and Brax didn't care, as long as Josie was happy, so they just tied the knot, and we had a dinner for them at Uncle Caleb and Aunt Brynna's place."

I nod and sit quietly, watching the scenery as we

drive toward Dom and Alecia's property. And when we're finally there, Keaton finds a place to park in the designated area and cuts the engine.

"Okay, let's do this," he says as he pushes out of the vehicle. I wait for him to open my door, but before I can hop out, Keaton cages me in and pushes toward me to kiss me, long and slow. The kind of kiss that's full of promises of what's coming later.

When he pulls back, I smile at him. "What was that for?"

"I probably won't be able to do that for a while, so I had to get it in now."

He winks and helps me out, and with my fingers laced through his, we make our way to the party.

"I don't want to cry."

Maya dabs at her eyes and sniffles as the five of us, Maya, Gray, our parents, and me, stand in the room that was designated as the *Groom's Suite*.

"There's no reason to cry," Gray says as he loops his arm around our sister's shoulders. "I want everyone to enjoy the day."

"It's already amazing," I assure him. "I think everyone's here because the chairs are all full out there."

"I just went to kiss Stella," Mom adds, dabbing her own eyes. "And she's just so lovely. I'm so excited for you."

"Ah, Mom, don't cry."

We do the family hug thing that we've done since I was a little girl, all huddled together.

"The most important thing is to be happy," Dad says softly. "Enjoy each other. Listen to each other. Don't take anything for granted."

Gray doesn't reply, and after a couple of sniffs, I announce, "Okay, it's getting mushy in here."

"Come on," Maya says, taking my hand. "Let's go find our seats."

Mom and Dad hang back with Gray for a minute. I know that Gray will escort Mom to her seat, and Dad will walk behind them.

The area under the tent, where Stella chose for the ceremony space, is so beautifully decorated. Pink flowers are sprayed over pretty much everything, and the most beautiful arch erected where Gray and Stella will stand is also covered in those pretty flowers.

I find Keaton and sit with him, while Maya finds her seat one row ahead of me, and before long, the music starts.

Gray and our parents walk to the front, and he kisses each of them on the cheek before standing with his best man, Vaughn.

Who looks like something out of a movie.

Because it's Vaughn Barrymore.

Then, it's time for Olivia to walk down the aisle. She's the matron of honor, and the only one standing up for the bride because she and Stella are lifelong best friends, and there are so many other women in Stella's life, she simply couldn't choose.

And, of course, everyone understood that perfectly.

Finally, the music changes and we all stand to watch the bride being escorted by her dad.

I don't think I've had any conversations with Nate McKenna before, although I have met him. He's tall and broad, with long dark hair and a stern face.

But today, that face is softer, full of emotion, and when Stella leans in to whisper something to him, Nate's mouth tips up in a smile.

I don't think there's a dry eye in the place by the time they reach Gray.

Before Nate gives Stella away, he shakes Gray's hand and pulls him in for a hug. Then, he kisses Stella on the cheek and then on the forehead.

It's the sweetest thing I've ever seen in my life.

"THIS IS A *PARTY*," Liam announces as he joins Drew, Keaton, and me at our table. He's breathing hard from some vigorous dancing. "Too bad it's not a live band. You and Uncle Leo could play."

"I'm relieved that it's *not*," I reply. "This way, there's no pressure."

"I have a question," Haley asks, clearly just a little tipsy.

"Shoot," Keaton says to his sister.

"Why are threesomes just for sex? Why can't I join a couple's argument if I want to?"

That stuns the three guys speechless for a moment, and then I look around the room.

"Who's arguing?"

"No one, it's just an observation," Haley says with a laugh. "Like, maybe I'm in the mood for a good fight. Or maybe I just want to watch a movie and snuggle. Why does it always have to be about sex?"

"Let me get something straight," Keaton says, his voice deadly now. "Did someone invite you to join a fucking threesome?"

"No." She rolls her eyes. "Jesus, I'm not that lucky. You're all too sober. I'm going to find Erin."

She wanders off, and I can't help but laugh. These people are *fun.*

"You've been quiet," Keaton says to Drew, who looks up and shrugs, drinking his soda. "What's wrong with you? Do you hate the new job already?"

"You started?" I ask. "That was fast."

"I'm transitioning," Drew replies. "And I don't hate it. But I met the new owners yesterday in a leadership meeting, and that was...*interesting.*"

"Interesting how?" I lean forward. "I want all the tea. Spill it."

"Both of them were there. Rome and London."

"Which one's which?" Liam asks.

"Rome is the guy. London's the girl," I inform Liam, who nods. "Keep going."

"They just don't know much about the sport," Drew continues. "And it's not a big deal, but I have a feeling that they're going to try to have their fingers in every-thing, and it's going to get old, fast."

"They own the team," Keaton says with a shrug. "They have every right to be in the thick of it. And, with time, they'll learn."

"I get it," Drew says. "I don't like it, but I get it. And London is just so...opinionated."

"About what?" I want to know.

"Everything. She wants new uniforms, which... whatever. We get new ones every year. But she wants the coaches to wear uniforms, too, and she'd like to help pick them out like she's a damn fashion designer."

"She is."

I grin when all three pairs of handsome eyes turn to me.

"What do you mean?" Keaton asks me.

"She's been in the fashion world, in some form or another, for years. She's especially fond of shoes."

"That explains a lot," Drew says with a sigh.

"How do you know this?" Liam leans on his hand, listening to me.

"Because I love fashion and shoes, too." I laugh when the three of them roll their eyes. "Stop it. It's not just a girl thing. I know plenty of men who love shoes. Anyway, it makes sense that she'd take an interest in that since she knows about it."

"It's stupid," Drew mutters darkly.

"Is she pretty?" Keaton asks and gets a glare from Drew. "Ah, I see. She's hot."

"She's going to be a pain in the ass."

"Not *your* ass," I point out. "You're not the head coach or the general manager. You probably won't have to deal with her much at all."

"She wants to attend my practices so she can *learn*." He takes a sip of his drink in disgust. "How am I supposed to get my shit done with some spoiled billionaire's daughter hanging out at my practices?"

"Good luck with that," Liam says, patting Drew on the back. "Keep me posted. Now, I'm gonna go dance."

Liam rushes off, and Drew continues to sulk into his drink.

"You need to cheer up," I say. "You still have your dream job, and you're making good money, I'm sure. She'll lose interest after a while. Or she'll learn everything she can and move on to the offensive coach."

"Let's hope," Drew says with a sigh. "And you're right. I still have a sweet deal."

"You're such an optimist," Keaton says to me with a grin. "Come on, sunshine girl, let's dance."

"I won't turn that down."

But Keaton doesn't lead me out to the dance floor. He bypasses it completely and drags me away from the party altogether, to a little building nearby.

"I thought we were going to dance."

"Oh, we are." He looks around to see if we're being watched and then tugs me inside.

From the quick glimpse I get of the room, it looks like wine barrels are stored in here. Likely empty ones.

And suddenly, Keaton lifts me, braces my back against the door, and kisses the hell out of me. This isn't deep and slow; this is *fierce*. This is *I haven't had my hands on you all day, and I'm about to change that.*

"What is it about us and weddings?" My voice is breathy and hitched as Keaton reaches down to unfasten his pants and doesn't bother to move my panties to the side.

He simply rips them off me.

"I guess I didn't need those."

"I need to be inside of you." *His* voice is just this side of a growl, and it only makes me want him more. "Jesus, I've been watching you all fucking day, so damn beautiful in this dress, so fucking classy and sweet, and all I could think about was sinking inside of you."

"Then do it."

He doesn't have to be told again. He pulls out a condom, rips the foil, and handles the protection. He's not gentle when he pushes inside of me, but I don't *want* gentle right now. I want fast and hard, and that's exactly what he's giving me.

"Damn," I mutter, my hands braced on his shoulders as he continues to push harder and harder. "Yes. Jesus, yes."

"Mine," he mutters against my neck. "Mine."

God, I love the way he *claims* me in moments like this. As if he's leaving his mark on me, warning off anyone else that might dare even give me a look.

It's sexy as fuck.

"Go over." He bites my shoulder, just the way he knows I love, and I quiver around him. "Damn it, go the fuck over, Sidney."

I couldn't stop if I wanted to.

And I definitely don't want to.

I cry out, and he covers my mouth with his hand to keep me quiet.

That's only hotter.

And when we're both spent and recovered, he lowers me to the ground and grins.

"Thank God for condoms," I say, breath still heaving. "Because otherwise, I'd have a mess on my hands."

"I kind of like the idea of you walking around with me inside of you," he says with a shrug.

"No. That's a *mess*. And I'm in a short skirt. No thanks."

He just snickers, tucks himself away, and before he opens the door, he leans in to kiss me, soft this time.

"I love you."

My heart flutters with those three little words, and I can't help but wrap my arms around his neck and hold on tight.

"I love you, too."

"It's damn early," I grumble as I reach over to answer my ringing cell. "Why are you calling me at seven in the damn morning, Annie?"

"It's nine here," she replies easily. "Wake up. I need you to be with it for this conversation."

"Then you should have called two hours from now."

I sit up and wipe the sleep from my eyes. Keaton walks into the room with a mug of coffee for me.

*"Thank you,"* I mouth to him and take a sip. "Okay, what's going on?"

"That song you put out on social media? 'Little Miss'?"

"Yeah?"

"It's blown up big time and caught the attention of everyone in Nashville. Babe, we're getting calls from all the labels, including the assholes who let you go."

"Wow, that's great." Awake now, I walk to the foot of the bed and slip on Keaton's T-shirt, then to the dresser to get some underwear. "Okay, I'm not naked anymore. I feel better about this conversation."

"That makes two of us. Honey, you've been invited to sing 'Little Miss' at the ACMs this Saturday in Dallas. Janelle Turner had to back out of the show because of a family emergency, and they want you to fill in."

My gaze whips over to Keaton, who's sitting on the bed, listening to every word.

"Wow, that's awesome. Of course, I'd love to. I can do it."

"Hell yes, you can. I'll email you all the details. I'll be in Dallas, as well, so we'll talk more about contract offers when I can see you in person."

"Wait." I rub my hand down my face. "The popularity of songs doesn't last forever, Annie. Should we move on this now?"

"I hear what you're saying, but I think we can talk about it in a couple of days. I'll have more information by then. Can you come to Dallas early on Friday so we can have some meetings then, before rehearsals?"

"Sure."

"Great. Expect an email from me within the hour. Have a good day, Sid."

And with that, she hangs up, and I just stare at Keaton.

"Shit's happening," he says with a soft smile.

"Yeah." My stomach starts to jitter with butterflies. "I *knew* that song was a hit."

"It's a fucking fantastic song. Leo will be stoked."

I nod and set my phone aside. "I'm going to ask you a question, and I probably already know the answer, but I have to ask anyway."

His eyes sober, but he reaches for my hand.

"Will you *please* come with me?"

Keaton sighs and slowly shakes his head. "I support you, 100 percent. I know you're going to kill it. But I can't go with you, Sid. I'm sorry."

"I understand." It's the truth. I really *do* understand. Keaton has some kind of horrible anxiety when it comes to this stuff, and the fact that we're able to work this relationship out at all is a miracle. "Like I said, I had to ask."

"I'm seriously proud of you," he says and brings my hand up to his lips. "So fucking proud."

"Thanks." I grin and then do a little shimmy. "Do you think it's too early to call Leo?"

"Probably. But you should do it anyway."

# CHAPTER 16

## KEATON

"I don't know what to wear," Sid says with a deep sigh. "I didn't know I was doing this, so I didn't have time to have a dress made for it."

"You don't have *anything* that hasn't been seen on TV or been photographed?" I ask her.

"I do, but they're in Nashville. Wendy!"

She grabs her phone and starts talking a mile a minute when her housekeeper answers the phone. After a few minutes, Sid hangs up and grins at me.

"You're a genius."

"I didn't do anything."

"You gave me the idea to call Wendy. She'll send a couple of things to Dallas for me to choose from. She's overnighting them, so they should be at the hotel when I get there tomorrow. That works perfectly."

"Do you want to practice the song again?"

"Aren't you sick of it already?"

I laugh and shake my head. "I know you want to get a lot of practice in before the show. I don't mind at all. Besides, you're hot as hell when you sing."

"Then, yes." She moves her head from side to side, as if her neck is bothering her, so I move up behind her to give her a little neck rub. "Oh, that feels like heaven."

"Don't stress about this, babe."

"Of *course*, I'm going to stress," she says as my fingers dig into her shoulders. "More than the contract opportunities, I want to make Leo proud. And, yeah, I know that's silly because he's already thrilled that the song is doing so well, but I can't help it. I wrote a song with my *hero*, and fans love it. I don't want to screw anything up."

"You won't." I kiss the top of her head and then walk to the piano. "Did your musicians get the music you sent them?"

"Yes, and they're ready to go. They're also flying in early for extra rehearsal time tomorrow."

"It's going to be a busy weekend for you."

"I love these weekends," she admits with a grin. She glances down, and I can see what she doesn't say in her eyes. She wishes I'd go with her.

But I *can't*.

"Okay, from the top." With her guitar in her lap, she begins the song, and I join in, playing with her.

The truth is, I'm not sick of the song at all. I *love* this song.

Sidney stops in the middle of the bridge and frowns.

"What's wrong?"

She narrows her eyes and whispers something under her breath and then runs from the room and returns with a notebook.

"I just got an idea for a new song."

"In the middle of *this* song?"

"Happens sometimes." She's writing furiously. "I'm going to play a melody. Do you think you can learn it?"

"I can try."

For the next hour, we play, tweak, and she writes notes.

"This is gonna be a good one," she says and sets her notebook aside. "Thanks for humoring me."

"You have to pay attention when the muse strikes, right?"

"Yeah. It shows up out of the blue most of the time. You know what? I think I'm ready."

"I know you are."

"Then I'm going to set this aside for now and enjoy the evening with you because it'll be close to a week until I see you again."

"You'll be gone that long?"

"I might have to jet over to Nashville if I need to sign contracts and pose for photos, give a press conference, that kind of thing. But we'll see. I'll keep you posted."

"Do that." I reach for her and pull her into my lap,

here by the piano. "What are your plans for this evening?"

Her smile is slow and satisfied. "Let's go to the bedroom, and I'll show you."

~

"HAVE A SAFE FLIGHT." Standing on the sidewalk in front of the departures at SeaTac, I pull Sidney in for a tight hug.

"I'll text you when I land." She lifts her face for a kiss, and I press my lips to hers. "Don't forget to watch."

"Are you kidding? I wouldn't miss it for the world. Have fun."

She grins now, clearly excited about the whole thing. "That won't be hard. See you soon. Love you."

"Love you."

She grabs her suitcase, and, rolling it beside her, walks into the airport, and I drive away from the terminal.

I have plenty of work to keep me busy over the next week while Sid's gone. I'm never *bored.* But damn, it's going to be lackluster and quiet without her around.

Once at my house, I shoot off some emails, putting out feelers for that Charger Vaughn wants. I'm just about to head out to the shop when my phone rings.

"Hi, Dad."

"What are you up to today?"

"Just working, but nothing big going on. What do you need?"

"Well, there's this movie…"

I can't help but smile. There's *always* a movie, but when you've been in the film industry for as long as my dad has, and own your own production company, it makes sense.

"I don't act."

"Ha. Funny. Actually, it's a period piece, set in the 1940s, and I need automobiles for it."

"Aren't there people who do that?"

"Of course, but they aren't my son. You don't have to come up with the actual vehicles, but I'd like your opinion on what to use. No one knows more about anything with an engine than my kid."

How can I resist that? "Yeah, okay. Where do you need me?"

"My office, if you don't mind. If you don't want to come into the city, I can meet you at the house."

"I can come into the city. I'm used to it by now and can drive it with my eyes closed. I'll be there soon."

"Thanks, buddy."

It's Friday morning, so the drive into the city isn't a fast one, but I eventually park in one of the family-only spots under Dad's building and ride the elevator up to his office.

When I walk in, I'm surprised to find that it's not just me at this meeting.

My sister, Liv, is here, along with several other staff members that I recognize.

"I didn't realize this was an official meeting."

"This is more efficient," Dad says and gestures for me to sit in a chair. "Liv's here to talk costumes, and Dean and Patrice will take notes and figure out how to put it all together."

"No pressure," Dean says with a smile.

"I'm *so* excited about this project," Liv says, practically dancing in her seat. "Fashion from the forties is just so beautiful. What's the storyline?"

"I don't think your fashion is going to be particularly glamorous," Dad says and begins to outline the plot. The characters aren't wealthy—in fact, it's the opposite. It's a poor family, figuring out life post World War II.

"It's still going to be awesome," Liv murmurs, jotting down notes.

"Vehicles will be interesting," I interject. "Not a lot of middle- and lower-class vehicles survived from that era, but I'll do some research and send you lists of what the family might have used."

"That would be great," Patrice says, raising her head from her iPad. "What about bicycles? And were motorbikes a thing then?"

"They were, yes. I'll send that info, too. Where is this being filmed? I can likely find vehicles for you, depending on where you'll be."

Patrice emails me the specifics for filming, and I already have some ideas about where to start for this.

It won't take me long at all.

Dean and Patrice leave to make their calls and do the research that Dad has given them, and Liv stands, as well, her nose still stuck in her iPad.

"I'll have drawings for you next week," she says to Dad and then turns to me and grins. "Welcome to the family business."

"Nope, I'm an independent contractor."

"You'll be back." Liv winks and then sails out of the office, closing the door behind her.

"I hear that Sidney left for Dallas this morning."

I narrow my eyes at my father. "Did you invite me here to talk about my girlfriend?"

"No, I needed your expertise for a project. But now we can talk about your girlfriend. Why didn't you go with her?"

"Because I don't want to have anything to do with that life, and you know it. I've never lied to anyone about that."

Dad shakes his head and walks to the wall of windows facing the city. "Why?"

"Why what?"

He turns back to me now. "Why won't you have anything to do with Sidney's life?"

"I didn't say—"

"That's exactly what you're saying. She can't change

who she is, Keaton. What scares you so bad about the fact that she's a celebrity?"

"I'm not *scared.*"

"Bullshit."

I stand and ball my hands into fists, more than a little pissed at my old man. "You made it clear my *entire* goddamn life that nothing good can ever come from being a celebrity. That the press is only out to ruin everyone. You kept us here in Seattle, far removed from that life, and you did everything in your power to keep us away from it."

"In my opinion, Hollywood isn't the right place for kids," he agrees. "But you're not a kid anymore, Keaton."

"The one time I dipped my toe into that world, it blew up in my face."

"Yeah, by a miserable, entitled little brat, who isn't even *in* the industry anymore. Who cares?"

I just stare at him. "I can't believe you're having this conversation with me. You're the one who always told us to stay away from the public life."

Dad blows out a breath and pushes his hand through his hair. "Listen, *I* don't do well with the spotlight. Even now, it unnerves me. Back when I met your mother? I had panic attacks at just the *thought* of being photographed."

"Yeah, I know. That's how you met Mom. I'm still shocked that she gave you a chance after you pretty much assaulted her at Alki."

"You and me both. But the point is, that's my issue. And yes, I protected my kids and my wife from that life because it was *crazy* for me. I had stalkers and women threatening to kill themselves if I didn't meet with them."

"Whoa."

"Yeah, it was a bitch. I was, and still am, grateful for the opportunities that came to me thanks to the movies I did when I was very young, but they really took a toll on my mental health. So, yeah, I might have overcompensated a bit with my kids."

"Or, you know, a *lot.*"

He shrugs. "I'm not sorry for that. However, you're not me, Keaton. You're a strong, levelheaded, intelligent man who's fallen in love with a fabulous woman who just happens to be talented and famous."

I don't reply.

"You *do* love her."

"Yeah." Now I'm the one to push my hand through my hair. "Yeah, I love her so much I can't see anything *but* her."

"And she loves you."

I nod and sit in the chair once more. "She loves me."

"Then you need to work this piece out, for both of your sakes. Because this relationship is brand-new, and you drew a line so deep in the sand, it'll come back to bite you in the ass. There are going to be moments that happen in her career when she'll want you by her side.

And you should be there, Keaton. You have to accept *all* of her."

My head whips up to stare at him. "That's what her dad said, too. And I know you're both right. I've just resisted it for so long that the thought of diving into that life is intimidating."

"You don't have to dive into the deep end. You just have to be open-minded. Don't be such a stubborn ass."

I sigh with a nod. "I don't want to disappoint her over and over again."

"Then don't. Let her have the spotlight, but be there to hold her hand. That's what your mom did for me, and it made all the difference in the world."

I lick my lips and stand. "Thanks. It might be next week before I get this movie stuff emailed over."

He raises an eyebrow.

"I have to go to Dallas."

"That's my boy."

## CHAPTER 17

### SIDNEY

"*A*s always, the majority of your money is going to come from touring," Annie says as we sit next to each other at the table in her hotel suite, looking over contracts. "The royalties from songs and album sales are standard. They want to release the album no later than this fall."

"That's only a few months away."

"Which means you'll immediately go into the studio," she says. "So, you'll be coming back to Nashville right away, of course."

"No."

Annie lifts a brow and sits back in her chair, watching me.

"I can record in Seattle," I add. "I can use Leo Nash's studio. If I need to go to Nashville to finish things up, that's fine, but there are studios outside of Nashville."

Annie makes a note. "I'll take that back to the

KRISTEN PROBY

studio. I don't see why they wouldn't agree to that. It happens more and more now that technology is what it is."

"Is that number my take *per show*?" I blink at all the zeroes. I've done relatively well in my career so far, but it's not easy to make a lot of money unless you've hit the *big time*. That number is on par with people I've admired for *years*.

"It'll fluctuate a bit with the size of the venue and such, but yes, that's your take. Minus my 10 percent, of course."

"Of course." I shake my head. "All of this because I wrote one song with Leo Nash?"

"It's a damn good song. This is about to be a huge turning point in your career, Sid. I can feel it in my bones, and my bones are never wrong."

"No, they're not. Wow."

This is exactly what I've always wanted for my career. Now I just have to figure out how I'm going to make it work with Keaton.

Right now, I feel torn. Because I want him, too, but I don't know how I'm going to do it.

And I don't like feeling as if I have to choose.

"Why aren't you turning cartwheels? I busted my ass on this."

"I know. I *am* excited! Maybe I'm a little over-whelmed, too. I wasn't expecting this at all."

"Okay, let's sign."

I hold up my hand and offer Annie an apologetic smile. "I need to think, just overnight."

"For fuck's sake, Sidney, what's to think about? This is as good as it gets. And if you sign today, you get all the label perks tomorrow at the show."

"That's really nice, but I need to make some phone calls. You know I trust and appreciate you. It's not that at all. I just need, like, twelve hours."

"Okay." She holds her hands up in surrender. "Let me know when you're ready to sign. Because I know for a fact that you won't turn this down."

I give Annie a hug before I leave her room and walk down to mine. I'm already tired. I spent about two hours rehearsing with my band, and then I met with Annie, and my mind is swimming.

I don't know what to do.

And I don't feel like I can just call Keaton and lay this all out at his feet over the phone. The last thing I want to do is make him feel guilty about something that he can't control. That's not fair, and I'd be pissed as hell if he pulled that shit on me.

Gray's on his honeymoon, and I refuse to interrupt that.

So, I call Leo.

"Hey, Sid. What's up?"

"Hi, Leo. Look, I'm sorry for suddenly calling or texting you all the time. I promise I won't make a habit of it."

"If I didn't want to talk to you, I'd send you to voice mail. Don't worry about it. What's going on?"

Much to my surprise, I tell him everything. All my concerns and what Annie just offered me.

And when I'm done, Leo's quiet on the other end of the line.

"Did you get sick of me and hang up?"

"No, I'm absorbing. And, I hope you don't mind, but Sam heard, too."

"I definitely don't mind."

"Honey," Sam says in that husky voice that I've always thought was hella sexy, "have you talked to Keaton about this?"

"No, you're my first call. I don't think it's fair to dump this on him."

Sam snorts. "You have to be honest with that kid. Look, you don't have to choose here."

"I don't?"

"Hell no," Leo adds. "I was always based out of Seattle after I met Sam. Luke's in Seattle, as well as several other members of the family who have fame. The cool thing about being famous and being the one making the label all the money is, you get to call some shots, shortcake."

"Did Leo Nash just call me *shortcake*?"

"You're short," he says.

"Leo's big on nicknames," Sam puts in. "And he's right. Don't sweat this. Sign that unbelievable contract and chase that career of yours, honey. You've totally got this."

"Thanks." Breathing a sigh of relief, I say my good-byes and hang up the phone.

I hope they're right.

SO FAR, the awards have gone well. According to the producer, we're ahead of schedule, which makes her very happy because going over the time slot costs money. I guess the speeches have been short and sweet.

I'm behind stage, ready to go out and perform. Scarlett Kincaid is announcing the winner for best country song of the year, and then I'm next.

"And the award goes to…'Knockin' Boots', song-writers Misty McIntyre, Bob Gillmore, and Rusty Davis."

"Holy shit!" I bounce on my heels, clapping and losing my mind. "Oh, my God!"

I watch the monitor as Misty, with tears in her pretty eyes, climbs the steps to the stage to accept the award, and I have to actively fight not to cry as she gives her speech.

"…and, of course, to my bestie, Sidney Sterling, who I think is backstage right now, for always being my rock and biggest cheerleader…"

"I love you!" I call out, even though I know she can't hear me.

When Misty is escorted backstage, we have time for a quick hug while the commercial break happens.

"I'm coming to your suite tonight," I promise her. "And we're gonna drink all the champagne in Dallas."

"Hell yes. Holy shit, I won!"

With the biggest smile on my face, I walk to the edge of the stage.

It's pitch dark, just like we planned. We decided to make this feel intimate, with me on a stool with my guitar, the piano next to me, and the rest of the band in the background.

To start, I'll sit on the stool, and the spotlight will hit me, and then when the piano joins, that light will come up, and then the rest of the band.

I think it's going to be super cool.

With a twinge of regret that Keaton isn't here, I walk out, guitar in hand, and take my seat.

I miss him. I know this isn't his thing, but I so wish he was here, even if he was just back at the hotel, waiting for me to get back later.

But I don't have time to think about that anymore when I'm introduced, and the spotlight comes on.

I start to play my guitar, singing the first few lines of 'Little Miss', and I'm absolutely shocked to see that many of the people in the audience are singing along.

The song is brand-new, and industry people already know the words!

Rick is in the audience and winks at me, singing

along. I see Annie beaming, sitting next to Misty. Even Dolly's here tonight, and she's smiling at me.

God, what is this life?

When the piano joins me, that light comes up, and I glance over and feel my heart stop.

It's a good thing that I know this song inside out, and I'm used to surprises while performing, because I'm staring at Keaton.

*Keaton is fucking here!*

And he's playing the piano with me while I sing.

He just grins at me, looking cool as a damn cucumber as we make our way through the song. When the rest of the band joins in, all the lights come up, and there's a round of applause from the audience.

*Little Miss do it all*
*Little Miss cannot fall*
*Little Miss get it done*
*When you want to run*
*No more having fun*
*And your life is on the line...*

I watch his fiery green eyes as I belt out every note of this song that I love so much, and when it's all over, the crowd stands, the applause deafening.

But then, to my utter shock, Keaton stands and walks around the piano to me. He's not mic'd, but I can hear every word he says when he kneels before me and pulls out a ring.

*Holy fucking shitballs.*

"Marry me," he says. "I love you so much, and we can make anything work. Be mine forever."

I cover my mouth as the applause explodes all over again, and then I hug him and plant my lips next to his ear.

"Of course, I'll marry you! Holy shit, this was a big step for you."

"Yeah, well, don't get too used to these grand gestures because I'm shaking like a leaf. But I'm going to try, Sid. For you."

He kisses me hard, and then we hurry off the stage so the rest of the show can continue.

"So much for being ahead," I hear the producer say, but I don't care. I can't stop grinning.

"You have so much to tell me." I glance down at the ring on my finger and feel myself swoon. It's so perfect, with a simple, round diamond on a platinum band. "And this is gorgeous."

"There's a seat next to her for you," someone says to Keaton. "You can go back to the audience now."

"You're going to sit with me?" I stare up at this man, and I can see the nervousness on his face. The slight hesitation. "You don't have to."

"Yes, I do. And I'm fine. Just don't leave me."

I laugh and lace my fingers through his. "No way. You're stuck with me, Mr. Williams."

~

THE AFTER-PARTY HAS BEEN the *best*, and I've been to some fun parties lately.

But this one? I'll never forget it.

Keaton and I are sitting at a table with Trisha and Garth. Garth's asking Keaton about cars, and from the little pieces of conversations I'm picking up on, it sounds like Keaton has another celebrity client in his back pocket.

Keaton always says that he's so proud of me, but I'm just as proud of *him*.

When I reach for my drink, I can't help but notice the sparkle of my ring in the light, and when I stop to admire it, I hear Misty giggle behind me.

"Don't mock me. I'm a newly engaged woman, and I'm entitled to ogle this beast."

"Mock? Me? Never." She sits next to me with a sigh and plops her statue onto the table in front of her. "That thing is *heavy*."

"Yeah, what a burden. Do you need me to take that off your hands?"

"Touch it and die." She grins in that smug way she has, then steals my drink and takes a sip. "Keaton's hot. How did you keep that a secret?"

"It wasn't a secret." I glance over at him, feeling a little thrill run through me. "It was just fast. And unexpected. I'm signing a new contract tomorrow morning."

"*Sidney!*" Misty tugs me in for a huge, celebratory hug. "Hell yes. HELL YES! I knew it was only a matter of time. I'm so fucking happy for you. Also, how did you wrangle a songwriting sesh with Leo fucking Nash?"

"He's Keaton's uncle."

I grin as Misty simply goggles at me.

"You're going to be *related* to Leo Nash."

I blink at her. "Yeah, I guess I am. Uncle-in-law. Also, Luke Williams will be my father-in-law, and Will Montgomery is another uncle-in-law. There are a million celebrities in that family; it's kind of mind-boggling."

"Holy shit." Misty swallows hard and then grins at me. "Good for you. How's Mama?"

I just love this woman. She always asks about my mom.

"She's doing really well. *Really* well."

"Thank goodness. This new life looks damn good on you, friend."

I glance at Keaton again and find him watching me with those hot, green eyes.

"Yeah. Yeah, it does."

## CHAPTER 18

### KEATON

"*I knew* it!" Liv shrieks and because she's on video call, we can see her do a little happy dance. Vaughn's just grinning at us. "I knew this would happen if Stella and I set you two up. We're *so* good at this!"

"Uh, Liv? I don't want to burst your bubble, but—"

"Let her have it," Vaughn suggests. "She's going to tell the story that way anyway."

Sidney giggles beside me and rests her head on my shoulder. "I was *so* surprised. I was on that stage, singing, and when the lights came up on the piano, there he was. I thought I was going to pee myself."

"We watched it," Liv says. "It was *so* romantic. It's all over social media now. Sorry, baby brother, but your days of being anonymous are pretty much over."

"Yeah." Surprisingly, I'm not as uncomfortable with that as I thought I would be. "She's worth it."

"I understand," Olivia replies with a soft smile. "And I get a new sister. You guys need to come back to Seattle so we can start making plans."

"Whoa," I reply with a frown. "We've been engaged for all of six minutes."

"Exactly," she says. "We're already behind. Have fun, you two. See you soon."

We end the call, and I sigh, looking down at the woman I'm going to marry.

"That was only call number one out of about twenty. This is going to take all night."

"How about this?" She scoots to face me. Her eyes are heavy with fatigue, but they're also full of excitement and love. The way she looked at me on that stage made me feel about twenty feet tall, and I immediately knew that it was the right call. "Let's call our parents, and probably Gray, and we can leave it at that until we get back to town. You know that everyone will want to get together anyway, and we can tell the story then, though they probably already saw it on TV."

"I think that's the only way we'll get some private time tonight, so I love that idea. But before we make any more calls, what *is* our plan for the next few days?"

She frowns, thinking it over. "Well, I don't *have* to go to Nashville because Annie has the contracts with her that I can sign."

"Wait." I hold up a hand and stare at her. "You're signing a *contract*? You failed to mention that to me."

"Oh, yeah. Sorry. I was so caught up in being asked to marry you that I forgot to mention it. And then we were at a party, and—"

I press my finger to her lips. "Skip to the good part."

She grins and bites my fingertip.

"No changing the subject."

She laughs and straddles me, wrapping her arms around my neck. "Annie and I met yesterday. I have a contract with Sony Nashville. The money is *good*, much better than I've received in the past. But it's going to be touring that really pays off. Keaton, I *have* to tour."

"Duh. I don't know if you know this, but you're a fucking big deal."

But she doesn't smile. She frames my face in her hands and watches me out of worried blue eyes.

"There will be times that we're apart."

"And there will be more when we're together."

She licks her lips, clearly very worried about this.

"Babe, you know who my uncle is. I grew up watching him and my aunt Sam deal with touring and all the things that come with that life. I'm not afraid of it."

"I think there are going to be a lot of details that we'll have to figure out. And I know that we *will* figure them out."

"Good because, for a second there, I thought maybe you were getting cold feet."

She simply kisses me, pressing her sweet lips to my

own, and sinks in, comforting both of us in a way I didn't realize I needed.

"Never," she whispers fiercely, tipping her forehead against my own. "No regrets. No cold feet. We'll figure it all out."

"Damn right, we will. Now, let's get back to the original question. What's our schedule?"

"Would you *like* to come to Nashville for a day or two, to see my house there and stuff?"

I guess I'd better, given that we'll be living there. "You bet. How about this? Let's hop over to Nashville for a few days, then stop in at your parents' place on our way back to Seattle so we can spend a few days with them."

"You'd do that?"

"They're your family. I think they're going to want to congratulate you in person."

"Us. They'll want to congratulate *us*."

"Right. Us. So, let's do that and then go to Seattle for a bit and figure everything out."

I don't want to put my house up for sale. The shop is just too perfect, and there's nothing that says that I can't work out of there whenever Sid's touring and I can't be with her.

It's all about compromise.

"Okay, I like this plan." She smiles smugly and pushes her fingers through my hair. "Maybe we should make those calls before I get you naked."

"Oh, you think *you're* going to get *me* naked?"

I cock an eyebrow at her and reach back, over the globes of her ass, thanks to the fact that she had to hike that short-as-fuck dress up around her waist to be able to straddle me.

"I think I've got an advantage here."

I push a finger inside of her, and she sighs, closing her eyes.

"Get those pretty blues on me."

She obliges and watches my face as my fingers play her like an instrument.

"Holy." She groans and lets her head fall back. "Shit."

The calls can wait.

I reverse our positions on the hotel bed, laying her flat on her back, and work her panties over her hips and toss them on the floor.

"Wait." She quickly clambers off the bed and wiggles her way out of her dress. "Sorry, this thing isn't pliable, and it digs into my back if I lie down."

She finally shucks it off, and I am met with the happy realization that there's no bra under it.

"Resume the position."

"Yes, sir." She offers me a mock salute, jumps on the bed, and lies on her back, her legs spread without any hesitation or self-consciousness at all.

I fucking love it.

"I don't know if I've mentioned this…" I unbutton the white shirt I wore to the show slowly. I shed the tie and jacket at the party earlier. Sid's eyes dilate, and she bites her lip when I let the shirt fall off my shoulders and to the ground.

Her eyes always immediately fly to my stomach.

She has a thing for abs. No pressure or anything.

"Mentioned what?" she asks.

"You're the most beautiful woman I've ever seen in my life." My pants follow the shirt, and I walk to the edge of the bed and reach for her soft foot. "Everything about you turns me on. Your sweetness, your love for everyone around you... The way you can sing like a goddamn angel."

I kiss the arch of her foot and then the ball of her ankle.

"These legs are a gift from heaven above."

"That could be a line in a song." She gasps when I kiss the inside of her knee. "You have a *really* good mouth on you."

"All the better to kiss you with."

I leave hot, wet kisses on the inside of her thigh, inching higher and higher.

"What else do you love about me?"

That makes me pause and kiss the crease where her leg meets her center. "The smell of your skin. The smell of your pussy."

Leaning in, I lick her from bottom to top, and she squirms on the mattress; her fingers dive into my hair, and she holds on *tight*.

"I love every curve on your body. Every line. Every dimple and dent. Even this scar right here."

I brush my finger over a white line on her hip.

"Stabbed myself when I fell off my bike as a kid."

"Ouch." Pushing myself higher, I lick that healed wound. "And when you look at me with those hot blue eyes, the way you are now? It makes me fucking crazy."

"How am I looking at you?"

"Like I hung the moon, and you want to fuck me until I pass out."

She nods. "Yeah, that's accurate."

"I also love that I don't know everything. That I get to learn more about you, and I have all the time in the world to do it."

"You know why?" she asks with a satisfied smile as I continue kissing my way up her body. I drag my tongue along her collarbone and then settle between her legs and brush my nose over hers.

"Why?"

"Because you're gonna *marry* me."

"Damn right, I am."

"Is that your only garage?" I ask as I point to the attached two-car space at her house in Nashville. We just arrived, and I met her driver, who picked us up from the airport and brought us here. He gave me the stink eye, but by the time we got out of the car, I won him over.

I'm glad to know that Sid has people who look out for her.

"Yeah, but it's pretty much empty if you want to take it over."

I nod, my mind already whirling. Sidney's house is nice and on the outskirts of the city with lots of trees that make it feel private.

"Whose car?" I ask her as I follow her to the front door.

"It's Wendy's." She smiles back at me, clearly happy to be here. I can tell that she loves this place, and I can see why. It's really nice. Sid opens the door and calls out, "We're here!"

"Oh, I'm *so* happy you're home."

A tall, slender woman with brown hair and a sweet smile hurries from the back of the house and immediately wraps Sidney in a big hug. Her eyes find mine over Sid's shoulder, and she winks.

"This is *him*."

"Wendy, I'd like to introduce you to Keaton Williams. My fiancé."

"Your fiancé," Wendy echoes with a grin. "Well, get over here. I'm a hugger, sugar."

Her southern accent is sweet, and she pulls me in for a motherly hug, then pulls back and frames my face in her hands. "I know this face. Why do I know this face?"

"He looks a lot like his dad," Sidney says. "Luke. Luke Williams."

I pause. This has always been my life, being introduced as my father's son. I'm not as angry about it as I was when I was a teenager, but it's still not my favorite thing.

My eyes narrow, and Sidney raises an eyebrow.

"Oh, yes, I see it," Wendy continues. "I enjoy your father's work very much. But I have to say, I'm a bigger fan of yours, since you clearly make my girl so happy. Welcome home, both of you. I have some food in the kitchen, and everything is clean and fresh for you. I'll head out so you can enjoy some alone time and settle in."

Wendy winks at Sid.

"He's a hottie. Good going, honey."

And with that, she leaves out the back door.

"Why did you look mad when I told her who your dad is?"

I shake my head, but she grabs my hand and squeezes. "No, really. That obviously pissed you off."

"No, it's just an irritation. I've always just been known as Luke Williams's kid. I'm proud as hell of my dad, don't get me wrong. But you're engaged to *Keaton*, Sid."

"Obviously." She frowns but then shrugs. "Okay, I'm sorry. I didn't realize that was a hot button for you. It won't happen again. Come on, I'll give you the grand tour."

The house is well taken care of and honestly beautiful. My mom and sisters would be in love with it.

Especially the kitchen.

"This is fancy," I say as I lean on the counter.

"I've seen way fancier. Like, at your parents' house," she says with a smile. "But yeah, I wanted a really nice kitchen. Wanna know a secret?"

"Of course."

"I've never cooked a meal here. Not once. But Wendy uses it all the time."

I cross my arms over my chest and grin at her. "Your secret's safe with me. *Can* you cook?"

"Oh, sure. My mom's a great cook, and I learned from her. But it's just me, and Wendy usually leaves me meals in the fridge. I'm not here a lot, so buying groceries feels like a waste because most of the food ends up going bad before I can eat it."

"I get it. Cooking for one is hard."

"But now I get to cook for *two*."

"I can help," I offer. "I know my way around a kitchen. My dad's an excellent cook, and food was always a big deal in our house."

"I finally get to use my kitchen," she says with an excited little dance. "But, for the record, *you* have a gorgeous kitchen, too. So, we'll have a good time cooking no matter which city we're in."

"That's a good point."

I can see myself living here. I can always buy more

shop space. Hell, there might be space in her backyard to build something, for all I know.

I'll miss my family, but I'm not going to sell my home in Seattle. We'll spend time both here *and* there.

It's not what I ever expected for myself, and it's not ideal, but I can make it work.

Sidney's worth it.

# CHAPTER 19

## SIDNEY

*H*e's been...different since we left Dallas. We spent three days in Nashville, and we still laughed, made love, and enjoyed each other. He was super sweet to my friends, and he swore up and down that he loved my house.

He never said anything to make me think that something was wrong.

But I can feel it in my stomach.

Something's off, but I don't know what it is, and it's driving me a little crazy.

I've asked him several times, but he insists he's fine.

I don't want to be one of those annoying women who nags and nags until their partner gets frustrated and blows up with *I'm fine!*

Keaton rented a car at the airport and turns into the driveway that leads to my parents' house. It's a beautiful day in northern Idaho, with bright blue skies and a slight breeze that carries the scent of early summer flowers.

It's my favorite time of year.

"It smells good," I announce as I step out of the car and turn to smile at Keaton.

"It's a nice day," he agrees, pulling our suitcases out of the back of the rented SUV.

Before I can say anything, the front door opens, and Mom and Maya come rushing out of the house.

"Get over here so I can hug you," Mom says as she hurries toward me. She's not wobbly on her feet *at all.* She looks just like she did ten years ago, healthy and vibrant, and it fills my heart with so much joy that tears spring to my eyes.

"Mom, you look fabulous."

"I feel fabulous." She wraps me up in her arms and holds on tight. "I'm so proud of you and excited for you."

She pulls back and gestures to Keaton.

"Get over here, son-in-law."

Keaton laughs and wraps his arms around both of us, and finally, Maya joins us, too.

"We're a pile of people in the driveway," I say at last, making everyone laugh. "We should go inside and get settled."

"Absolutely," Mom agrees and loops her arm through mine as we walk to the door.

"Where's Dad?" I ask her.

"Oh, he was indisposed," she says with a wink,

implying he was in the bathroom. "He'll be out in a few minutes. You two look happy and exhausted."

"I'd say that's accurate. It's been a busy week or so."

We walk inside, and I can't believe my eyes.

Standing in the living room is my father, and both of Keaton's parents, too.

"Oh, my God!"

There are more excited hugs and laughs, and when I glance over at Keaton, he looks happier than he has in *days.*

*What is going on with him?*

Is he having second thoughts?

I really need to have a talk with him.

"We had to come celebrate with you," Natalie says with a smile. "I just couldn't wait any longer to give you both a hug and get a look at that ring."

"Oh! Here." I hold my left hand out so all the women can get a good look at it. "He did a *good* job."

"Now, that's a *rock*," Mom says with a laugh. "How can you hold your hand up with that much weight on it?"

"It's a burden I'm willing to bear."

"Good job, Keaton," Natalie says and then pulls me in for another hug. "I'm so happy for both of you."

"Thanks."

"Have you two thought about where you're going to live?" my dad asks.

"Seattle," I immediately reply.

"Nashville," Keaton says.

My head whips to him, and I scowl. "What? No. Absolutely not. We'll be based out of Seattle, Keaton."

The parents and Maya seem to back away, leaving Keaton and me to hash this out.

"Your job and your house are in Nashville," he points out. "I'm not going to ask you to give that up."

"Who said anything about giving it up? I'm not selling the house. It'll be there when I need to go to Nashville for work, but I can do most of it in Seattle. I can use Leo's studio, and we can live in *your* house. I like your house, but please, for the love of Moses and all the Greek gods, let me decorate it."

"Amen," Natalie mutters.

"Wait." Keaton holds up a hand and shakes his head. "How did we communicate so badly on this?"

"Is *this* why you've been so distant? So…different?"

"I'm not trying to be. I'm just working through everything in my head because there's a lot to do when it comes to getting my business set up in Tennessee and moving everything out there."

"No." I shake my head and hurry over to him, wrapping my arms around his middle. "That's not happening. I didn't ask for that, and I won't. Before you proposed, I already decided that I'd be making Seattle my home base. I *like* being closer to my family. Nashville is the office. The Pacific Northwest is home."

He frames my face in his big hands, hope so fierce in his green eyes that it makes my heart hurt for him. I hate that he's been agonizing over this.

"I'm sorry we didn't talk about this," I continue. "You were worried about nothing."

"I wasn't *worried*," he insists. "Home is wherever you are, sweetheart. But, I admit, I'd rather live in Seattle and go to Nashville when you need to, or even when you want to."

"That's my plan." I grin up at him, and then, even though we have an audience, I push up to my toes and kiss him. "We can have *both*, babe. We don't have to choose."

"Hell yes." He kisses my forehead and then hugs me close as the others start to talk in excitement.

"And you're okay with the fame?" The question comes from my dad, but Luke nods in agreement.

"I photograph well," Keaton says with a thoughtful nod. "I've been told that I'm handsome like my dad. I think it's all going to work out just fine."

Luke grins, and my dad laughs.

But Keaton looks down at me. "It seems I'll do just about anything to be with your daughter. Even pose for pictures in uncomfortable clothes."

"We'll have to beef up your wardrobe just a smidge."

"Why do I get the feeling you just want to go shopping?"

I grin up at him. "Duh, because that's my favorite sport."

With a mischievous grin, he leans down and whispers in my ear. "I think what we did this morning is your favorite sport."

I feel my face flush and plant my elbow in his side.

"Be good."

"Honey, I'm *very* good. And I plan to spend the rest of my life reminding you of that."

"Lucky me."

# EPILOGUE

## SIDNEY

*E*very woman in the Sterling-Williams-Montgomery, and all the other surnames, clan is in my house tonight.

*Our* house, that is.

Mine and Keaton's.

And let me just say, that's a *lot* of people, but how could I narrow down who to invite to help settle my nerves the night before my wedding? Who would I leave out?

No one. Because I love every single one of them, even the ones I don't know so well yet.

I have a lifetime to forge relationships with everyone in this big, crazy family.

More than anything, I'm *so* happy that my mom and sister are here with us. Keaton's dad flew them in a few days ago, along with my dad, so they were here to help me get ready for this shindig.

Even though it's a *very* small affair, right here at the house—only including our families and a few good friends—means there are close to a hundred people in town for the wedding.

"This family kicks ass," Misty says as she joins me on the front porch. "Will y'all adopt me?"

"Sure." I grin and pat the spot next to me on the porch swing that Keaton hung for me last week. "Have a seat."

"What are you doing out here by yourself?" Misty sits and takes my hand in hers, linking our fingers together. "The party's inside, and you're the guest of honor."

"I just needed some fresh air, that's all."

Misty takes a deep breath. "You'd never know that y'all are so close to the city. It feels like you're out in the country here."

"I know. It's one of the things I love about it. It's so quiet, but within ten minutes, I can be at all the shops and restaurants I want. Keaton chose a good spot."

"He also chose the right girl."

I grin over at her. "Yeah, he did, didn't he? Thanks for taking a break in your schedule to come to Seattle for this."

"Are you freaking kidding me? Your best friend only gets married once. Well, maybe twice, but I wouldn't miss the first one for the world."

We laugh at that until our sides hurt.

"I'm not doing this again. He's the one for me."

We hear loud laughter coming from inside, and we smile at each other.

"What are they doing in there?" I ask her.

"Well, when I came out to find you, they were just getting ready to play a drinking game, but with Jell-O shots."

"I didn't have any Jell-O shots."

"I think Keaton's aunt Samantha brought them. She's married to Leo, right?"

"Yeah. Well, let's go get some Jell-O shots."

When we walk inside, I'm surprised to find that it's just the aunts and moms, including *my* mom, sitting in a circle on the living room floor, with a heaping platter of shots sitting in the middle.

"Never have I ever had sex on a tour bus," Jules says and then points and laughs when Sam reaches for a shot.

I wade my way in and pluck my own shot off the top, making everyone roar with laughter.

"Atta girl," Meg says, offering me her hand for a high five, and then we all laugh when Misty also reaches for a shot.

"Where are the others?"

"Oh, the young ones are out in Keaton's shop, listening to music and doing who knows what." Natalie gestures to the general area of the shop, and I feel my eyes go wide.

"Keaton specifically said we're supposed to stay out of there."

"Since when do the women in this family do as they're told?" Stacy asks. "Okay, moving on. Never have I ever had sex in a cemetery."

I don't wait to see who takes a shot on that one, but I hear someone exclaim, "Jeanie!" and I do *not* want to know about my mother's cemetery sexcapades.

"Your mom—" Misty begins, but I cut her off with a shake of my head.

"Not going there. No way."

Misty laughs as we make our way to the shop, where I can already hear the music and laughter coming from inside.

And when I open the door, I sigh in resignation.

"Y'all are trying to get me divorced before I even get married."

Stella looks my way and grins. "We're not touching *anything.* We're just sitting on these blankets, eating snacks, and talking about sex, I promise."

"Just so you know," I inform them all and point to the cameras up in the corners of the building, "Keaton's watching every move we make in here."

"He'll be bored," Liv says and pats the spot next to her on the blanket. "Come on, sit with us. You too, Misty. Get in here."

"Don't have to ask me twice." Misty plops down next to Stella, accepts a glass of champagne, and digs into a bowl of chips. "Come on, Sterling, don't be a party pooper."

"I'm not a party pooper," I reply and sit next to Liv,

then glance around this big circle. All of these women are amazing, and as of tomorrow, they'll all be my family, whether by blood or marriage or friendship.

"You're getting sloppy," Maya says, shaking her head. "I can see sentimentality written all over your face."

"Nah, I'm just thinking that I'm one lucky bitch, that's all." I shrug a shoulder and then eye my sister. "So, now that Mom doesn't really need a full-time care-giver anymore, maybe *you'll* be having sex."

"From your lips to God's ears," Maya says, raising her glass in cheers.

"What *are* you going to do now?" Stella asks her, and my sister just shrugs.

"I don't know, honestly. Maybe I'll travel a bit here and there. We'll see."

"I'm just glad that your mom is doing so well and has made such a huge turnaround that she doesn't *need* to be watched all the time," Sophie says. "That's awesome. There are at least a dozen homes owned by our family all over the world. You should try to visit each one of them."

"I couldn't ask your family to—"

"I'm sorry," Stella says, holding up a hand. "That's *our* family. And I think that sounds like the most fun thing I've ever heard of. We'll figure it out."

Liv glances over to the garage bay behind me and points. "That must be my husband's car."

I look back and then nod. "Yep, that's the Charger."

"It looks haunted," Haley says, and that makes us all laugh.

"Keaton will make it look brand-new," I reply proudly and notice that Liv gets a sly smile on her face. "What?"

"I'm totally going to have sex in that car."

"For sure," Haley agrees. "Just not while it still looks haunted."

"Are you ready for tomorrow?" Chelsea asks. She's the youngest of the Williams family, and she and I have become close over the past few months.

"I'm past ready. I moved past ready about a month ago. Now, I just want to get it over with so I can finally be his wife, and we can get on with it."

"How did you manage to keep the press away?" Sophie asks. "We're not even at the vineyard."

"As far as I know, no one told the press," I reply. "Which is just how we all want it."

"I want to see the dress," Haley announces, standing up. "Let's go inside and swoon over it again."

"Let's go!" Stella and Liv reach for the bottles of champagne, and everyone files out of the shop to the house, much to my relief.

I'm the last one to leave the building so I can shut off the lights and lock the doors behind me. But before I leave, I look up at the camera and smile.

I don't know if he can hear me, but just in case, I

say, "Don't worry. I've got this. I can't wait to marry you tomorrow. I love you."

I blow Keaton a kiss, then turn out the light and shut the door, locking it behind me.

Tomorrow afternoon can't get here soon enough.

ARE you excited for Drew Montgomery and London Ambrose's story? They are up next in The Stand-In!

You can get all of the information here: https://www.kristenprobyauthor.com/the-standin

# BONUS EPILOGUE

## NATALIE WILLIAMS

"*Y*ou're home." My husband's arms come around me from behind as I stand at the kitchen counter, and I lean back against his hard chest and let out a breath I didn't realize I was holding.

"Got here a little bit ago," I confirm. "I didn't want to wake you."

"I was waiting for you." He kisses the top of my head, and then I turn in his arms and look up into eyes so blue they could make the gods weep. And still, all these years later, they still hold all the love and all the passion they held when I first met him. "Why do you look sad, baby?"

"I'm not sad." I shake my head, but the tears still fill my eyes. "Melancholy, I guess. He's my only boy, Luke, and now I have to pass him over to another woman."

"Hey." He pulls me in for a big hug and rocks me back and forth.

Yeah, I got home earlier, but now, in Luke's arms, I'm *really* home.

"He's still your boy," he says softly.

"He's a man." I sniffle and then shake my head once more. "And this is silly because I love Sidney. She's just the sweetest woman, and I know she loves my boy so much, but how did this happen? How did they all grow up so fast?"

"I don't know." He glides his hands up and down my back, soothing me. "It feels like it was the blink of an eye. But at least they're not going far. They're ten minutes away."

"Thank God."

I blow out a breath and pull away from him.

"I was going to make some tea. Would you like some?"

Luke looks at something over my shoulder, and then he slowly smiles and shakes his head.

"No, I'm going to head to bed. Have some tea with your boy." He kisses me softly, and then he turns to walk back toward our bedroom, and when I turn around, I see Keaton standing ten feet away.

"I thought for sure you'd be dead asleep," I say as I move to fill a kettle with water. "You have a big day tomorrow."

"I don't like sleeping without her." The comment is

283

so easy, so simple, that it takes my breath away. My Keaton is so much like his father.

"That's lovely," I reply and pull two teacups out of the cupboard. "Let's have some tea, then, and we can talk."

Keaton came to stay with us tonight because it's bad luck to see the bride before the wedding, but he wasn't happy about it.

"I saw that the girls hung out in my shop tonight."

I smile and unwrap the tea bags.

"I don't think they did any harm."

Keaton shakes his head and sits on the stool on the other side of the kitchen island. How many times have we been here, just like this, over the years? A hundred? A thousand?

One of our favorite things to do when Keaton was a kid was to stay up late, after everyone else had gone to bed, and make chocolate chip cookies.

"You know what would go good with the tea?" I raise my eyebrows in surprise because it looks like he was thinking about the same thing I was.

"Cookies?" I ask, and he just grins. "I have some premade dough. Let's do it."

I busy myself turning on the oven and placing the dough on a cookie sheet, and once the cookies are in the oven, I turn to my son and sigh.

"I'm not ready for you to get married."

Now it's his turn to raise his eyebrows. "You don't like Sid?"

"No, silly, I love her to pieces. I'm not ready for you to marry *anyone*. It's a mom thing, I think."

"We won't be far away."

"That's what your dad said, and you're both right, but it's not the same."

I come around the island and sit on the stool next to him as we wait for the cookies to bake, and I rub my hand over his strong, broad back.

My boy is a handsome man.

"Are you ready for tomorrow?" I ask him.

"I would have eloped the day after she agreed to marry me if she'd have gone for it. There's nothing in this world that I want more than her. Nothing I *love* more. Does that sound cheesy?"

"Only in the best way. That's exactly how you should feel when you're about to get married. Like the sun rises and sets with the person you're in love with."

"I know that was how Dad felt about you," he says and turns to me with a rueful smile. "Hell, he still does. It's pretty gross."

"It's pretty wonderful from where I'm sitting. I'm so glad that you have parents who showed you and your sisters what it means to have a loving marriage. Have we had our rocky moments? Of course, we're only human, and your father refuses to put anything in the dishwasher. But love and respect? We have that in spades, and you guys saw that."

"You're right," he says, nodding. "And I think because we *did* see it, the four of us know not to settle for anything less. How do you feel about being a grandma?"

My heart stops. All the blood drains from my body.

"Holy shit, is Sidney pregnant?"

Keaton grins. "No. She's not pregnant. But I want kids, Mom. I want a lot of kids."

"You little shit." I slap his arm as he laughs, and then the oven timer goes off, so I stand to get the cookies. "You got my hopes up on purpose."

"You're the one who jumped to conclusions. But, hopefully, it won't be long before we start having babies."

"What about her career?" I ask as I remove the hot cookies from the pan and walk back, around to set the plate between us.

"What about it?"

"I would expect that it would be difficult for a woman to maintain a successful music career *and* have a bunch of babies."

Keaton scowls and stares down at his cookie. "Sid and I talked about it, and we'll make it work. We can always hire a nanny."

"Or a grandma." I wink at him and bite into a cookie. "We all had fun tonight at your *home*. Sidney's turned that place into a cozy, lovely place to live for both of you."

"Yeah, she's had a good time with it. And you helped."

"It was my pleasure. I'm going to get mushy for a second, so bear with me, okay?"

"You wouldn't be my mother if you weren't getting mushy."

I grin and take his hand. "*You* have been the pleasure of my life. You and your sisters, your father, our family. You are everything I ever wanted, and I couldn't be prouder of you, Keaton. You are my sweet, quiet boy, and you've turned into a wonderful, strong man."

"Yeah, really mushy," he says as he stands and pulls me into his arms for a long hug. "I love you, Mama."

And here come the tears again. But they're happy tears.

"I love you, too, baby."

# THE SOUNDTRACK

All songs written and produced by Josiah and Rachel Holien.

## Life in the Slow Lane

Small town girl
    Born and raised in the country
    Turned eighteen and packed up for the city
    Lived my dream out for a couple good years
    But it's funny how now
    I'm crying homesick tears

I drove miles further than I ever dreamed
    Played dress up for anyone who'd hear me sing
    I drank fancy wine and took shots of fame
    But never thought I'd ever miss the days
    Of life in the slow lane

Traded a starlit night with a city high rise
    From karaoke bars to being the headline
    A black limousine replaced my old white truck
    I guess you gotta build a home
    Wherever your heart ends up

I drove miles further than I ever dreamed
    Played dress up for anyone who'd hear me sing
    I drank fancy wine and took shots of fame
    But never thought I'd ever miss the days
    Of life in the slow lane

I miss those dirt roads I used to ride
    Before the fast lane ever caught my eye
    I should have taken my sweet time
    And listened when they said life flies by

I drove miles further than I ever dreamed
    Played dress up for anyone who'd hear me sing
    I drank fancy wine and took shots of fame
    But never thought I'd ever miss the days
    Of life in the slow lane

## Moon Shine

Whether it's the whisky
    Or the moonlight
    That draws me to you

I don't want to sober up
    I pray the sun won't come up
    In case I lose this view

The shine of the moon against your lips
    Intoxicating moonshine bliss

Moonshine
    Getting drunk on your love and I better
    Think twice
    Before I kiss another man in the
    Moonlight
    But you make me feel like I'm home again
    In the moonshine

I want to drink in this moment
    For as long as I can
    You got me holding my breath
    Heart pounds in my chest
    As you hold my hand

The shine of the moon against your lips
    Intoxicating moonshine bliss

Moonshine
  Getting drunk on your love and I better
  Think twice
  Before I kiss another man in the
  Moonlight
  But you make me feel like I'm home again
  In the moonshine

I thought that love like this was a myth
  Like the man on the moon
  But I think that I found him when I found you

Moonshine
  Getting drunk on your love and I better
  Think twice
  Before I kiss another man in the
  Moonlight
  But you make me feel like I'm home again
  In the moonshine

## Good Girls Gone Bad

You said you liked good girls
    So that's who I tried to be
    You said you liked blonde girls
    Now my hair smells like bleach

You've always told me what you like
    Saying I'd probably be your type
    If I did all these things to change my life
    For you

But now I kiss you and wish you
    The time of your life
    Go enjoy your side piece
    While the real Queen claims what is mine

And maybe someday you'll realize
    Just exactly what you had
    But never again will you hold me
    Cause this good girl's just gone bad

Don't tell me you're sorry
    Cause there's no going back
    And don't you try to call me
    Cause this line just went dead

I won't bat an eye when you're all alone
    And the good lord knows

I wont pick up the phone
You can leave your message at the tone
We're through

But now I kiss you and wish you
The time of your life
Go enjoy your side piece
While the real Queen claims what is mine

And maybe someday you'll realize
Just exactly what you had
But never again will you hold me
Cause this good girl's just gone bad

You aren't worth another night
You aren't worth one more fight
You're the good the bad and the ugly
Wrapped up in one selfish tragedy

Can't remember why
I ever wanted you so badly
But this good girl is gone gone gone gone
Gone gone gone gone gone gone bad

## Little Miss

You gotta be picture perfect
    If you want to try to make it
    So call me little miss counterfeit
    You won't know it's fake
    Until you examine it

Since when did real become the enemy
    When did faking smiles become enough for me
    My heart is worth more than your poisonous
    Standard of what perfection is
    I'm so much more than your perfect little miss

I'm tearing myself out of this chapter
    Pick another girl to pose in your picture
    Just call me little miss blank piece of paper
    I erased your lines
    And I'll write them better

Since when did real become the enemy
    When did faking smiles become enough for me
    My heart is worth more than your poisonous
    Standard of what perfection is
    I'm so much more than your perfect little miss

Little miss last picked
    Little missed chances
    Little miss move over

Little missed dances

Little misused heart
Who's done letting you
Pick her apart

Since when did real become the enemy
When did faking smiles become enough for me
My heart is worth more than your poisonous
Standard of what perfection is
I'm so much more than your perfect little miss
I'm so much more than your perfect little miss

# NEWSLETTER SIGN UP

I hope you enjoyed reading this story as much as I enjoyed writing it! For upcoming book news, be sure to join my newsletter! I promise I will only send you news-filled mail, and none of the spam. You can sign up here:

https://mailchi.mp/kristenproby.com/newsletter-sign-up

# ALSO BY KRISTEN PROBY:

**Other Books by Kristen Proby**

**The With Me In Seattle Series**

Come Away With Me - Luke & Natalie
Under The Mistletoe With Me - Isaac & Stacy
Fight With Me - Nate & Jules
Play With Me - Will & Meg
Rock With Me - Leo & Sam
Safe With Me - Caleb & Brynna
Tied With Me - Matt & Nic
Breathe With Me - Mark & Meredith
Forever With Me - Dominic & Alecia
Stay With Me - Wyatt & Amelia
Indulge With Me
Love With Me - Jace & Joy
Dance With Me Levi & Starla

You Belong With Me - Archer & Elena
Dream With Me - Kane & Anastasia
Imagine With Me - Shawn & Lexi
Escape With Me - Keegan & Isabella
Flirt With Me - Hunter & Maeve
Take a Chance With Me - Cameron & Maggie

**Check out the full series here:** https://www.
kristenprobyauthor.com/with-me-in-seattle

**Single in Seattle Series**
The Secret - Vaughn & Olivia
The Scandal - Gray & Stella
The Score - Ike & Sophie

**Check out the full series here:** https://www.
kristenprobyauthor.com/single-in-seattle

**Huckleberry Bay Series**

Lighthouse Way
Fernhill Lane
Chapel Bend

**The Big Sky Universe**

**Love Under the Big Sky**
Loving Cara
Seducing Lauren

Falling for Jillian
Saving Grace

**The Big Sky**
Charming Hannah
Kissing Jenna
Waiting for Willa
Soaring With Fallon

**Big Sky Royal**
Enchanting Sebastian
Enticing Liam
Taunting Callum

**Heroes of Big Sky**
Honor
Courage
Shelter

**Check out the full Big Sky universe here:** https://www.kristenprobyauthor.com/under-the-big-sky

**Bayou Magic**

Shadows
Spells
Serendipity

**Check out the full series here:** https://www.

kristenprobyauthor.com/bayou-magic

## The Curse of the Blood Moon Series

Hallows End
Cauldrons Call
Salems Song

## The Romancing Manhattan Series

All the Way
All it Takes
After All

**Check out the full series here:** https://www.
kristenprobyauthor.com/romancing-manhattan

## The Boudreaux Series

Easy Love
Easy Charm
Easy Melody
Easy Kisses
Easy Magic
Easy Fortune
Easy Nights

**Check out the full series here:** https://www.
kristenprobyauthor.com/boudreaux

## The Fusion Series

Listen to Me
Close to You
Blush for Me
The Beauty of Us
Savor You

**Check out the full series here:** https://www.
kristenprobyauthor.com/fusion

## From 1001 Dark Nights

Easy With You
Easy For Keeps
No Reservations
Tempting Brooke
Wonder With Me
Shine With Me
Change With Me
The Scramble
Cherry Lane

## Kristen Proby's Crossover Collection

Soaring with Fallon, A Big Sky Novel

Wicked Force: A Wicked Horse Vegas/Big Sky Novella
By Sawyer Bennett

All Stars Fall: A Seaside Pictures/Big Sky Novella
By Rachel Van Dyken

Hold On: A Play On/Big Sky Novella
By Samantha Young

Worth Fighting For: A Warrior Fight Club/Big Sky
Novella
By Laura Kaye

Crazy Imperfect Love: A Dirty Dicks/Big Sky Novella
By K.L. Grayson

Nothing Without You: A Forever Yours/Big Sky
Novella
By Monica Murphy

**Check out the entire Crossover Collection here:**
https://www.kristenprobyauthor.com/kristen-proby-crossover-collection

# ABOUT THE AUTHOR

Kristen Proby has published more than sixty titles, many of which have hit the USA Today, New York Times and Wall Street Journal Bestsellers lists.

Kristen and her husband, John, make their home in her hometown of Whitefish, Montana with their two cats and dog.

facebook.com/booksbykristenproby
instagram.com/kristenproby
bookbub.com/profile/kristen-proby
goodreads.com/kristenproby

CPSIA information can be obtained
at www.ICGtesting.com
Printed in the USA
BVHW041711130723
667207BV00001B/71